Queen Magic

Other Series by Sarah K. L. Wilson

Dragon School

Dragon Chameleon

Dragon Tide

Bridge of Legends

Tangled Fae

Empire of War & Wings
Book 5

Sarah K. L. Wilson

Published by Sarah K. L. Wilson, 2020

This is a work of fiction. Similarities to real people, places, or events are entirely coincidental.

QUEEN MAGIC
First Edition. December 8, 2020

ISBN : 978-1-7772645-4-3
Cover Art by Luciano Fleitas
Written by Sarah K. L. Wilson
www.sarahklwilson.com

For Cale,

Always.

THE LAST BOOK

Hot the fire, hot the flame,

Hot the light that on us came,

Hot the searing smoke and heat,

Hot the things the fires eat,

Our hot fire eats you up,

Can you drink this molten cup?

Our hot fire burns you down,

Will you ever earn that crown?

- Source Unknown, found scrawled on the rocks of Far Reach

CHAPTER ONE

Juste Montpetit's horse was a sleek bay gelding with an arched neck and he danced to the side as Juste tried to mount. The bay's nostrils flared and his eyes rolled back in his head. Juste whispered something to the horse that sounded more like hissing than actual words and the creature stilled, but I wasn't fooled. Just like me, it was only still because it must be still. Only quiet because it was that or die. Terror was not the same as calm – though both might make you motionless.

Juste flung himself in the saddle and sent a piercing glance my way. I couldn't help but avoid his blue eyes. They were far too much like Osprey's – bright and penetrating as if they could read my thoughts.

Instead, I fixed my gaze on the new crown he'd had made for himself. It was still moving. What magic was required to make a crown of asps that seemed to always be reweaving itself? Had they carved it directly from the Forbidding and then shaped it? I did not know, but as I thought those things, three snake heads on the crown turned, looked at me, and extended themselves as far as they could in my direction. I flinched away. Only Juste would make himself a crown as creepy as he was.

"Prepare to ride, Empress," Juste said, with a cruel twist to his smile. "We ride to the heart of it all. We ride to claim all of what is ours now."

"Isn't it enough to rule the Winged Empire?" I asked him, my voice rough with all the emotions I didn't dare let myself feel. My brothers' and sisters' deaths were still too raw. My terror for my little nieces and nephews too recent. I didn't dare let myself sink into those overwhelming waves. Didn't dare wonder if Osprey would be able to keep them safe. I didn't dare let my hands shake as much as they wanted to. "Why do you feel the need to conquer this, too?"

His bay danced over to me, and Juste reined it close until he could reach me. I tried to lean back, away from his touch, but he was too fast. His hand snaked out and grabbed my chin, yanking me forward and staring deeply into my eyes with his over-large blue irises.

"It's always been this, Empress," he said in a way that made me think of snakes hissing. All the heads of the black snakes that made his crown reached for me and I could have sworn one tickled the hair just above my forehead. "The Winged Empire was never the ultimate goal. I was always born to rule – to speak the fate of a man and see it come to pass. To lay out a plan and see a city fall or watch a rebellion crumble. And I'm good at it. I've taken what is mine. I've laid hold of my birthright.

"But that is only the beginning. I was born to rule everything. At the heart of that tangled mass – the Heart of the Forbidding – is the Seat of the Adder. And I will sit on that seat and all that is under the sway of that dark magic will be mine – and with it, I shall grasp and grasp until nothing in all the world is outside my reach. I shall take their sons and daughters. I shall run my hands through their piles of rubies and wrap myself in their silks. Their seas shall taste of the salt of the tears I bring, and their mountains will weep with their blood. All things will be mine – every pair of wings will fly to my bidding, every scale of the snake shall touch ground that is mine. And even you – you treacherous queen –

even you will delight in kneeling before me for I shall make it the only thing you have left."

His kiss, when it came, tasted of acid and I made sure to bite him again and turn the taste to blood.

He hissed, drawing back and his snarl showed his blood-smeared teeth. "You think you will keep me from you with all your biting. It's like you don't even realize it's what I want."

He shoved me as he released me so that I rocked in the saddle, spitting blood from my mouth and trying as hard as I could to keep the horror from my face. Each time he seized more for himself, his cruelty grew in proportion. How many more lives should he be allowed to ruin? How many more homes and cities?

I reached for my short sword and a hand slammed onto mine, pinning it against the hilt.

The Claw beside me clicked her tongue. "Nothing more than teeth for you today, Empress. I've been assigned your guard. I will never leave your side so that you never leave his. I will never let harm befall you – so that you can't harm him."

I put all my fury into the look I shot at her, spitting the last of the blood in my mouth so that it stained the pretty white embroidery on the sleeve of her uniform.

"What is your name?"

She seemed unaffected by either my fury or my spittle, though her sharply cut chin-length hair wavered a little from tension in her jaw as she spoke. "Claw Elodie."

"Of House?" I prompted.

"Nuthatch." She spat the word like she hated it.

I took a moment to adjust the Winged Crown on my head.

"I have orders that you are not to remove the crown," she said sharply.

I could already tell I was going to love having her at my side. "Aren't you a delight, Claw Elodie."

I peered around us at the group gathering. Four Wings – the one with the orange-tinted eagle spirit-bird, the one with the golden-tinted raven spirit-bird, and Wings Essena and Xectare. The two of them were watching me with predatory smiles as if this crown on my head would be no protection at all from how they planned to tear me to pieces and feed on my liver.

The manifestor of the orange-tinged eagle was a thin, hunched man in what I guessed might be his late thirties. He wore a pair of glass panels wrapped in thick wire and attached to the front of his face so that he had to look through them to see. How odd. He was already mounted on a brown mare.

Beside him, the woman with the golden raven sat on a black gelding at least two hands higher than the eagle-man's mare. She wore her white hair the same way that Elodie Nuthatch wore hers – chopped straight at the jawline. Her eyes were no-nonsense, and her dark face was lined with wrinkles.

Four of them plus Juste made it five manifestors versus one me. And my bees were exhausted, dulled to the faintest whisper.

Tension sang through me as if I was a string pulled in a bow. I felt their every movement and look in my direction. I felt their emotions twanging all around me. I felt like I might break at any moment.

Hold yourself together, Aella. You must not break. Skies have mercy. Stars have mercy.

I gritted my teeth. I would not let them see me worried about them.

On either side, the Claws were assembling in rows and a series of supply carts pulled by carabaos were being lined up behind us. Everyone worked in a hurry, half-breathless as orders were called out and people scrambled to obey.

Juste leaned in close to a pair of Claws with medals strung across their chests. Generals. He was leaving his orders with them. Both of them exchanged anxious glances – and no wonder. The countryside was aflame, the flames were spreading toward the city, their newly crowned emperor was leaving them in charge, and he was riding into that inferno. It was an insane situation. Just like everything else that had happened here since the Hatching Festival. I'd feel bad for them if they didn't oppose everything I loved. As things stood, I hoped they were so busy fighting fires that they couldn't think of rebels.

The last wagon was being chivvied into line when Juste raised his hand. Silence fell around us and the generals who had been speaking to him hurried away.

"Children of the Winged Empire," Juste said solemnly, standing in his stirrups so all could see him and his writhing crown. He looked so very young – and yet ancient in the ways of cruelty and power. "We ride today into the heart of the inferno. Do we ride for glory?"

He let the question hang in the air.

"Yes!" the Claws around me shouted, clashing swords against bracers. I hadn't seen them do that before, but I could see why they did. It sent a little thrill of anticipation down my spine even though I knew this was crazy.

They were all crazy.

"Do we ride for the honor of the Empire of War and Wings?" Juste asked, a little louder this time.

"Yes!" Another clash.

"Do we ride for the domination of our enemies and the conquest of all the world?" This time he was shouting.

"YES!" the chorus shattered through the air with the smash of metal against metal and my breath caught in my throat.

Whatever else I might want to say about Juste Montpetit, I had to admit, he knew how to inspire his followers.

"Ride with me, Children of the Empire." He sounded like a lover seducing his beloved. "Ride with me to our destiny."

He pointed forward and the party began to move, horses walking at first but once we were moving there was a jingle ahead and then the horses moved to a trot and Elodie finally let go of my fist so she could handle her reins.

Which left me somewhat free for the moment. Not free to ride away and escape, but free to plunge my sword into Juste's heart right now if I wanted to.

Maybe.

I maneuvered my horse with care, trying not to look suspicious. Trying to keep my face calm and serene as I brought my brown mare up alongside Juste and his wild-eyed bay.

"Already trying to kill me, wife?" he asked, his eyes never even glancing in my direction. My heart stuttered as he spoke my intentions aloud. "I think you should reconsider. It's not in your best interest to see me dead."

CHAPTER TWO

"And why would that be?" I asked, my heart in my throat as we raced down the street, our trot turning into a canter. Civilians scattered on either side of the road. Already panicked from the fires, they spread themselves against walls and packed into alleys to make way for the new-crowned Emperor and his entourage. Juste hardly seemed to notice them. His eyes burned hotter than the fires we rode toward.

"I am headed to the Heart of the Forbidding Wife. To the Seat of the Adder."

He'd said that before, but this time when he said it, a memory flickered up in my vision – a memory of a great, dark seat inside the jaws of something tangled and shredded. There was something odd about the seat … it had holes in it almost as if it was meant to drain some kind of fluid and under the seat, runnels were carved. Before it, a table was laid, but not with food, and around the table, other seats were set in place. The vision faded and I shook my head, squinting in confusion. What had that meant?

When I glanced back at Juste, he was smiling. "I knew that would bring a memory. What did you see, wife?"

"I saw a large black seat with tangled, shredded … something … around it. There was a table and there were seats for companions."

His smile grew in both size and satisfaction. "Yes. That's where we go. And when I sit on that seat, the Forbidding will withdraw and become mine, and everything it has touched will be mine, too. It will fit itself to my hand like a glove and I will make it dance to the flick of my finger and tear when I form a fist."

"And why would I want any of that?" I asked, grimly.

His eyes grew wide as if he thought it would be obvious. "The Forbidding will return those it has claimed – every life stolen, every father or mother or child claimed by its tangled magic will be set free. I thought you would want that. Have you not lost people to the Forbidding? Would you not want your dead returned to you?"

I licked my lips thinking of Osprey running from the Forbidding with my nieces and nephews with him. My siblings and their spouses hadn't been there. I'd known immediately that they had been taken by the dark magic. It was the only reason for them not to be there defending their little ones. Just the memory of that sent stabs of pain through me to the point where it was hard to breathe. Agony clawed up my throat, burning across my chest and my thoughts froze half-formed. I knew this grief. I knew it from when I'd seen my father killed. I knew it from when my mother's life had faded. It would hold me in its grip if I let it.

With great effort, I forced it aside. There would be a time for grief. That time was not now. I must keep my eyes clear and my mind on the game. I felt for my bees, for any trace of their buzz. Nothing replied to my inner call.

"You see what that would mean for you." He sounded pleased.

"The Forbidding is on fire," I said, hedging. "Nothing could survive that."

He shrugged. "So it would seem. But that doesn't negate what

I've said. I know you have lost people. I know you want them back. I know that you've fought this monstrous evil all your life. What would life here be like without it? What would hold you back from accomplishing everything you've ever dreamed of as a fledgling settlement?"

I gave him a long, dry look. "You?"

His laugh was harsh but truly amused. "Am I so much worse than the Forbidding that you would rather see it survive and me dead on this street?" He lifted a single eyebrow at me. "I am only a man. I am only mortal."

I wasn't sure that he believed those words. And yet, he was right. He could be dealt with later. He was only a man, but a chance to strike the Forbidding – to get back those who were lost …

A hunger began to rise in me, a desperate need I couldn't fully force back down. With it, the smallest tendrils of my overwhelming grief clutched at me. It would have me if I let it.

I sucked in a deep breath, trying to force it back, trying to cleanse it from my heart, but it would not budge.

"I see it in your eyes wife. I see that you finally see what I see. You finally want what I want. And I need you to accomplish it. The Hissan were very clear. We are both needed."

I met his eyes. Truth and certainty burned side by side in them. I swallowed down all my hate, all my fury, all my desperate desire and tried to think.

It was possible that I could kill him right now, however unlikely since I didn't have the element of surprise anymore. He was stronger than me. His magic was not depleted. He was a better swordsman than I was. I could also kill him later – when he slept or when another opportunity cropped up. I hadn't been able to do that before. Murder, it turned out, had been a line I couldn't make myself cross. But I thought I could do it this time. Now that I really knew what would happen if he lived – how many were bound to suffer and die at his hand. And if I did, then the madness ended. Someone else would rule. The martial law could be over. The drastic measures that curtailed my people – done. Even the Hissan could be ousted from the continent. All of that could happen.

And there would still be the Forbidding curling around our homes and towns – not just here anymore but across the sea to the main continent. It would always be a threat, always be a problem. I tried not to think of the siren song that was singing in my heart, you could get them back, you could get them back, you could get them back.

Instead, I tried to be objective. But it was hard to do. I'd spent my whole life fighting the Forbidding. I'd only been fighting Juste for a few weeks. As much as I hated him, as much as I wanted him expunged from the earth – I wanted the Forbidding gone more.

"No need to answer me," Juste said crisply. We were almost to the gates. "Your answer is in your face, wife. You know I must live to sit on that seat – and you will do your part to get me there."

"What part is that?" I asked coldly. I knew what he would say, but I needed to hear him admit it – admit he couldn't do this by himself and that he must let me live.

"Keep trying to remember. Keep showing me what you see," he said grimly. "Your part is that of the Oracle. It was meant to be mine, too, but you had wounded me too gravely to be blessed at the temple of the Hissan."

That must be what he told himself in the middle of the night when he remembered what a coward he'd been – how he'd made me stand in his place.

He patted his belly where the honeycomb was always exposed and clicked his tongue at me. "You and your troublesome bees."

I ignored the comment. We were riding through the gates now, and my stomach twisted into knots as the wave of overpowering heat whipped across our ranks, searing my skin as if I was standing too close to an open oven door.

"Now, stop distracting me, wife, and don't even think about killing me while I am vulnerable, or neither of us will see the world we wish for."

I hated him with every single thought of my brain, with every beat of my heart, with every twitch of my itchy fingers on the sword hilt.

But he was right. I would let him live. Because we both wanted the same thing in our own separate ways – we wanted Far Stones to be free of the Forbidding. We wanted this grueling, endless war to be over.

When the Claws at the front of our ranks began to steam, they stopped and Juste rode forward, hand held up to stop everyone else.

My horse followed his with Elodie tucked in tight beside me. I couldn't help it. I wasn't the type to hang back even if it seemed like a terrible time to ride forward.

Juste opened his mouth and for the barest fraction of a second, it almost seemed as if his jaw had unhinged and opened wider than any person's jaw could open. I shuddered at the same moment that the snake issued forth from his mouth, its inky black spirit-scales gleaming in the sun and shining a sickly green. It poured, and poured, and poured from his mouth, widening as it reached the ground and then widening still as it poured toward the fire. Juste made a choking sound when the last of it left him, as if he were vomiting the tail of the snake out of his mouth.

The snake surged forward and around it the fire quelled. It was as if someone had dashed water over the snake's path and far enough on either side that Juste could ride his wild-eyed steed in the "S" shaped trail left on the ground and not be burned. My mare followed close behind, her nose almost touching the tail of his erratic bay.

It was a moment before I realized I was the one urging her forward, unable to stop myself from wondering what came next. If I was going to die as the wife of the Emperor, I'd rather die riding my horse between the flames than die locked in a white cage. Frustratingly, Juste seemed to know that. He was betting on it.

The heat singed the edges of my golden dress and I smelled burned hair. It was a moment before I realized that the ends of my long curls and the ends of the horses' manes and tails were frizzled from the heat.

"No one can survive this," Elodie said with certainty in her voice. And for a moment, Juste paused, looking forward. Was he reconsidering his own choice?

I felt a little surge inside me, and a bee fell into my hand, buzzing wildly, and glowing a brilliant white-gold.

Juste chewed his lip for a moment, looking the most uncertain I'd ever seen him. Around us, were flames, rooted deep in dark tangles and sharp, shredded slivers of sky and grass, forest and path. We were within the embrace of the Forbidding and also within the flame. Within and within and within like a coin within a chest within a larger chest within a still larger chest. My brain kept echoing that word as if it should mean something to me.

COME WITHIN. I shook at the familiar voice of the Forbidding in my mind. LET US FOLD YOU WITHIN.

And then Juste shook his head as if he were dispelling a thought he didn't like, and his horse stepped forward.

And for just a bare moment, it seemed as if I was seeing two of him. One Juste that was stepping his horse forward and one Juste who had changed his mind and was going back, and beside that Juste rode another Aella with a haunted face and woebegone eyes and my bee fluttered through the air and settled on Returning Aella's head.

I blinked and felt that strange sensation of the undertrails – as if I was being folded. The sensation passed and the vision was gone. With a shiver, I let my horse step forward after Juste's.

CHAPTER THREE

If I had thought that walking through the gaps of the Forbidding was bad before, then this was worse. It was darkness and flame, smoke and the mind-bending warping of the Forbidding all tangled up into the kind of hell that made it impossible to say for sure whether we'd spent five minutes or five hours in the embrace of this dark magic.

The smell of smoke clung to us, searing our lungs until we could smell nothing else. I grew light-headed as it became more and more difficult to find untainted air to breathe.

We learned quickly that we all must stay close to Juste and the snake's trail. We learned it the first time when one of the carabao carts got stuck and the Claws tried to push it free. It wouldn't budge. A younger Claw, not much older than I was, tossed his cloak and weapons into the cart and strained to push it, his chiseled jaw and muscles bulging with the effort. Another Claw moved to join him and the first one shuffled down to the far corner of the cart – the corner that was off the snake path. He was there, pushing, one moment, his attractive face screwed up with effort. And then the next moment, he burst into flames. His eyes went huge, he shrieked, and was sucked into the Forbidding the way smoke is sucked up a chimney.

I don't think I was the only one who screamed. I do know I was the only one who Juste absently cuffed because of the scream.

"No weakness, Empress," he said viciously, before grabbing me by a chunk of my hair and dragging my face forward. "Eyes on what is before, not on what is behind."

Yes. I would think about what was ahead – cleansing this land of the Forbidding and then ridding it of Juste Montpetit.

I was beginning to feel the first stirrings of my bees again – not enough to call them, but a reminder that they were there. The only problem with that was that as my bees grew in strength, I could hear more of the Forbidding. Through the swirling flames on every side, it whispered to me.

FOLD YOU UP. WEAR YOU DOWN. FIND OUT WHAT YOU ARE.

Sometimes I couldn't make out clear words, but it mumbled on and on in my mind and left me shivering despite the heat.

"How long do you think you can keep this up?" I asked Juste. His strength was remarkable. We'd been traveling for what must have been hours – though the sun was hard to read between the walls of smoke and flame and even if the passing of time had been clear, I was certain that time would be warped here just as it had been in the gap trails. "Your strength will fade eventually and then the fires will consume us all."

He was leaning slightly forward, his shoulders hunched, and eyes glued straight ahead.

"Hoping for an easy end to all this, wife?" he asked, but his heart wasn't in his threat. He really was getting tired. Doubt tickled the back of my mind and left anxiety in its wake. "Hoping the flames will close in and consume me?"

"I think that no matter what I hope for, that is almost certain to be the case soon," I said, trying not to feel sick as I realized it was true. I was going to be burned alive. It was going to hurt worse than anything I'd ever experienced until I died.

I startled when I realized he was watching me instead of peering ahead, a slow smile spreading over his beautiful face.

"I like that expression. Do wear it often for me."

Was it my imagination, or did it feel hotter now? I wiped a bead of sweat from my forehead.

"If only my dear brother had lived to see that look of horror. I would have enjoyed his pain at seeing it even more than I enjoy yours right now. Unfortunately, I can't leave you imagining your doom and being driven mad by it – as much as that pleases me." He snapped his fingers and Elodie was right beside me before he even glanced behind him. "Make sure she doesn't fall from her saddle."

I looked at him with confusion and then he grabbed the neck of my dress and ripped it, exposing my chest just below my collarbone where his feather lay. He pressed his hand over the mark and a look of bliss filled his face.

The voice of the Forbidding silenced, the hum of my bees fled with it, and then my vision began to fade, and everything went dark.

I was seeing a vision – but I knew that it wasn't something that was. It was something that would have been if a different decision had been made. I watched Juste pause just as we were entering the Forbidding. I watched us turn around and go back to the city. Watched Returning Aella go with him. She drew her sword, trying to overpower him, and was clubbed over the head by Elodie. My vision flickered and she was in the cage in his throne room listening as he marshaled his troops for counter-attacks against the Single Wing. A bounty was to be placed on the heads of every member of her family.

When I truly awoke again, I blinked away those memories of a life that could have been. I was almost grateful to realize I was dripping with sweat, leaning on the shoulder of someone in a thick blue coat. Because it meant my family wasn't being hunted down. I wasn't in a cage.

I shuddered before I could compose myself.

It was Elodie I was leaning on. She shoved me upright. "If you're awake enough to open your eyes, you're awake enough to sit up on your own."

I managed – barely – to stay seated in the saddle of the mare. She was moving slowly now, barely able to pick up her tired hooves. Her breath was coming too quickly. This journey was going to kill the horses. It was going to kill us. It was still better than the alternative.

"Le Majest," Claw Elodie called through a hoarse voice. "She is awake. You could draw from her again."

I blinked my exhausted eyes, trying to make sense of what I was seeing. Claw Elodie's jacket was completely unbuttoned. She'd tied a cloth around her forehead to absorb the sweat. I teetered as I looked behind me at the horses that followed, their heads were barely above the ground, they sagged and stumbled like they may not have another mile of life in them. Many of the Claws had dismounted, stumbling beside the horses. They, like Elodie, had shed every scrap they didn't need and had cloths tied around their heads. My filmy golden dress felt too heavy. Its full skirt pulled at me, trying to drag me from the saddle and the crown on my sagging head only stayed on because someone had jammed it down so hard it wouldn't budge.

My only encouragement came in seeing the Wings stumbling,

too, their spirit birds flickering in and out of life over their heads.

"Yes," Juste said and his throat sounded raw. "Once more."

He stilled his horse and waited for us to catch up to him. He swayed in the saddle as he reached for me, but it was not his hand that touched me. He leaned over in the saddle and his eyes closed almost in reverence as he kissed his feather under my skin. I was too weak to push him away. Too weak to scream my defiance.

The world went dark again.

This time when I woke, there were fewer horses. Only Juste and me were still mounted. The carabaos pulled their carts at the very back of the line and between them and us, people stumbled on their own smoking feet. Beside my horse, Elodie shuffled, too.

We were all going to die like this.

"Not today," Juste muttered through blistered lips. When had they blistered like that? "Not today."

I felt something on my face. My brow wrinkled at the feeling. I knew that feeling. What was it?

My mind wasn't working correctly. I didn't even have the energy for sadness or anger. Not even for panic, though I was sure panic was the right response.

It took another minute for me to realize what it was. A cool breeze. Something ahead wasn't on fire.

"We should turn back, Le Majest," Xectare said from behind me, and by the tone of her voice, I thought that perhaps she had said this before – many times before. "There is no end in sight. It was a noble thought. But now, we fade. We die."

Juste paused for only a moment.

"Press on," I said, shocked by how raw my voice was. I didn't have the energy to say more. Didn't have the energy to explain that I was feeling a breeze.

My emperor husband looked into the distance, his eyes narrowing, his hands falling to the saddle in front of him and then he shook himself and his horse stepped forward again. And once more, a translucent vision version of him turned around and went back, and Exhausted Aella turned with him. He reached for her, to take what strength she still had.

I blinked the vision away and my horse followed after Juste. She was starting to fade. I could feel it in her movement beneath me. I hoped I wouldn't have to watch her die. My eyes pricked with tears – which was crazy since she was only a horse and I'd already lost so much more than that. But it was like I'd lost so much – so many people, so much of my heart – that a loss I should have been able to bear was just too much for me now. I crumpled in my saddle and I didn't realize I was crying until the tears began to hiss on my cheeks.

"Save your energy," Juste gasped. And then his horse stumbled and fell to its knees.

Under normal circumstances, Juste was graceful and light on his feet. In this case, he scrambled awkwardly off the horse's back, kicking up a cloud of soot into the air as he tried to find his feet. Elodie began to move toward him, but he waved her away.

"I need more from the Empress," he said, drawing his blade and stumbling a step toward us. "You must keep holding her up."

He turned, and with an awkward chop, he partially severed the horse's head – enough to kill it. But not cleanly. Not neatly. I gagged into my mouth.

Juste looked up at me, his face blank with exhaustion and

need. He slammed his palm against my chest and took. And everything was black again.

If I could have blocked out what I saw next, I would have. I watched Exhausted Aella – the one I'd just seen turn back. Her horse died under her. And then the Claws began to fall. I woke when she stumbled into the ash. A dark cloud of it puffed up around her. And then she was breathing flame. Her screams filled my mind.

Someone had slung me over my saddle, face down. I struggled to pull myself up and Elodie touched me on the head. Even her touch didn't have much power. She'd lost her jacket. Her white shirt was streaked in soot. So was her face.

"Don't bother looking up. I'll tell you. The horses are all dead but this one. So are some of the Claws. We have one carabao left. No cart. Only packs."

Her voice trailed off as if it, too, were leaving her.

But now what I felt was more than a breeze. I could feel coolness pulling at me, urging me onward. I could feel green things ahead. It was in my bones. It was deep in my heart.

"Almost there," I gasped. "I can feel it."

Elodie's laugh had no humor. It was as scalding as the world around us.

My horse stumbled under me. I fell from its back into the ash and felt the embers scald my knees and palms as I struggled to my feet. Thank the skies I'd kept my boots when they forced me into this filmy golden dress. I tried to smooth my hair out of my face and it tangled in my crown.

"They don't come off easily," Juste said wearily. I looked up to see him watching me dully as Elodie dispatched my horse. "You'd think the crowns would just fall off, but they don't. They become part of you. It's their magic. The magic that makes you more than a man, barely less than a god."

He sounded delusional. Maybe he was.

"I'm no man," I said dully.

"If you were, this wouldn't be so much fun." He sounded just as lifeless despite his threats.

And then the smoke parted up ahead and I saw it.

"Green," I said, stumbling to my feet. "I smell green."

CHAPTER FOUR

Juste was the first to stumble out of the flames onto the charred grass and then out to where it grew green and thick and waist-high. I couldn't tell if his gasps were relief or just the desperate attempt to breathe something other than ash and soot. He let his charred hands sweep through the long green grass, but he waited until the last of those still alive in our party cleared the flames before his snake winked out.

We stared around us like children coming out of a nightmare. I was the first to begin coughing, clearing my lungs of all that had been sucked into them. But around me, I heard others coughing and hacking, too.

"We'll rest here," Juste declared, slumping into the grass beside me. I fell to my knees, let my forehead fall to the ground, and closed my eyes as exhaustion crippled me.

As if it had been waiting for the right moment, the last of my bees – the one following Ixtap – sent me a sharp vision.

He was arrayed for battle and standing with his closest Hissan warriors looking over a field below us. The ranks of men behind him were arranged roughly in large rectangles with pennants featuring birds flying over their heads. But as my bee moved, looping around Ixtap, I saw an army of similar size arranged before them. And these men also had pennants. The largest pennant was red, though I couldn't make out what bird was depicted on it. Houses. The pennants must signify which houses were fighting under those banners. And if there were that many banners, then this was most of the Houses of the Winged Empire – on one side or the other.

One of Ixtaps's men rode up to him, leaping off the horse and making a snake sign as if it were the sign of the bird.

"They will not relent, Lord Ixtap. They say they will fight for this claimant to the throne. They say they do not believe that you stand for Le Majest Juste Montpetit. That if he wishes to make a claim, he should come himself. It has been months since anyone has heard from him. They say he must be dead."

Ixtap made a disgusted sound in the back of his throat. "And those who follow?"

"Will not be swayed. It is war, Lord Ixtap."

"Then war it shall be," he said, opening his hand and letting his snake flow from it. "Do not allow a surrender. We end this here."

I woke to a pair of green eyes looking at me. The wrinkles around them told me the eyes were considering what to do with me.

I sat up and the person drew back, tilting her head to one side. A quick glance around me told me that the rest of my party slept – exhausted – in the grass around me. We were surrounded by a ring of people carrying weapons – weapons that were familiar to me. The clothing was also familiar to me. Scale armor and snakeskin featured predominantly, and large polearms were in every hand. These were the Hissan – the people of Ixtap. And the woman in front of me was definitely their leader.

"You're the Hissan," I tried to say, but my voice came out as a squeak.

The woman snapped her fingers and one of her people broke from the line and brought me a waterskin. I drank gratefully.

The woman spoke and I knew she was speaking Hissan, but I could understand it because my mind had been tweaked by the Hissan all that time ago when I'd been at their temple. I shivered at the gruesome memory of that snake rummaging through my mind.

"You haven't had water for a very long time. It steals the voice. Don't drink too much or you will be ill."

"Thank you," I said.

She frowned and then without warning, a snake poured out of her ear and into mine.

"I hate it when you people do that," I said bitterly but now I could tell she understood me.

"You've met someone from among us. His snake made it possible for you to understand," she said, her eyes wide. There was a murmur from the watching crowd.

I cleared my throat. "Ixtap."

This time, the sound around me was a gasp.

"He and his followers left this place not long ago. Days, perhaps? Maybe weeks? Such a promising boy." Her eyes were wistful.

"Boy?" I croaked.

Her face seemed to fall. "Did he … did he seem much older to you?"

I looked at her carefully. I couldn't tell what these people wanted, but honesty was always the best course.

"He seemed about your age."

Her face paled. "My age?"

"Is something wrong?"

She shook her head and helped me to my feet. "Time works differently here. And usually, my people live outside the folds of the Forbidding to prevent it from altering us, but some of us volunteered to hold this outpost and that means living within it. It folds. It kneads. It warps the landscape, but it also warps time. Did it seem like very long to you? The time you spent walking through the Forbidding to get here?"

I glanced back at the wall of smoke surrounding the rolling grasslands we stood on. "It was less than a day."

Her face was hard. "Perhaps. But it seems like only weeks ago that I sent my son out into the world and now you tell me he is of an age with me."

Her son. I felt my jaw fall open and she nodded.

"And you arrive with a man wearing the adder crown. The crown my son swore to fit to the right head."

"He declared Juste Montpetit the Adder at the top of a temple," I said carefully. "There were tests."

She was nodding, her eyes bright. "There are always tests. But this time, one was found worthy."

Her words were breathless. She looked up at her people and I saw Juste's eyes open from where he lay on the grass. He didn't so much as twitch, but his eyes were watching her.

"The Adder has come," she said – this time loudly enough for everyone assembled around us. "The time of waiting is over. The time to cleanse the land has come!"

The circle responded with a loud whoop and Juste sprang to his feet as light as if he hadn't just passed through the Forbidding in a journey that might have taken us months to complete.

"So, let it be declared," he said calmly in Hissan, straightening his Adder crown. "So, let it be done."

If I'd thought the cheer was loud before, it was deafening now. How could he manipulate a crowd so well when he cared nothing for people?

My eyes stayed fixed on Juste even as the Hissan helped our people to their feet. They stayed locked on him as our helpers led us through the grass to where a hill rose in a perfect mound before us and to the open-topped tower that stood on the mound. The bottom of the tower was open, the top accessed by a winding staircase that spiraled around the whole structure. They began to prepare a feast the moment we arrived. And still, my eyes were locked on Juste. Because that was not triumph on his face. It wasn't joy. It wasn't even relief. I knew that look. He was counting and measuring, weighing and choosing. He was scheming. And his scheme had something to do with these Hissan and this outpost of theirs.

Was it something he had planned with Ixtap? Or was it something of his own?

I wished I could be sure he would stick to what he'd promised – that we were here to gut the Forbidding, but with Juste trust was a bad choice.

His words never gave him away. His manner was utterly polite and deferential. His orders to his people were to recover and rest.

He, himself, took a place in the shade and drank water and fruit juices and talked to the woman – Essa – of Ixtap and the wonders he had seen when he visited with him before. He spoke of Hissan fashion and weapons, of a game called Ichene, and of beadwork and foods, and all the time his eyes glittered with planning and ambition.

I watched him until I could stand it no more and I climbed the tower stairs instead. Elodie was resting her agonized eyes – burned from staring at the flames for too long. And since there was nowhere to run – since this outpost was completely surrounded by fire, held back only by the snake magic of the people who lived here – no one followed me, and no one tried to stop me.

The steps came out to the top of the tower where a low wall surrounded the platform. From here, I could see the fields surrounding the tower where there was just enough farmland for herds of goats and careful rows of vegetables and grains. Just enough to sustain the people who lived here. So why set up this outpost in the middle of the Forbidding? Why create this place? Our hosts had kept their mouths closed about that, and Juste hadn't seemed interested in finding out more from them.

I bit my lip and looked at the horizon. Every moment I spent here might mean days back at home. And I was missing it all. I thought of Osprey sheltering my nieces and nephews. I thought of the Single Wing and my siblings fighting for freedom.

Just like that, my vision waved and I saw Exhausted Aella dying in the ash again, saw her bee fly out to the world beyond to see the Forbidding creeping across the land and swallowing up Glorious Ingvar, swallowing everything clear to the sea.

I blinked and the vision was replaced by Returning Aella in her cage, watching as Juste lined up her family at a tall gallows.

"This marks the last of those who opposed me in Far Reach," he declared. "This land and all its inhabitants are the property of the Empire of War and Wings."

And then that vision as gone, too. I sagged as it left me.

Two possible other futures. Both terrible. Both worse than this one – maybe. I didn't know. I felt blind without my bees. How much time had passed out there in the world? In that time had I lost more of those I loved? It had to take a while for an army to form against Ixtap. How long? Weeks? Months?"

I chewed the inside of my lip and felt like I might vomit. My life was slipping between my fingers – and for what? We needed to find this Heart of the Forbidding. We couldn't afford to waste another moment.

"I'd offer a coin for your thoughts, but I've already given you a crown." Juste's voice pierced my musings and I spun toward his voice. Around us, darkness was falling.

"We need to get to the Heart of the Forbidding," I said. "Who knows how much time has passed since we left Glorious Ingvar."

"About three months, I would guess," Juste said casually.

I felt my jaw drop. "And how would you have calculated that?"

"I asked Essa a few questions about times and days and compared that to what I knew from Ixtap. But this is not our final destination," he said, looking out to where the distant fires still lit the skies. "To get there, this outpost must be stripped down. And it will burn. We leave at midnight. You might want to think about sleeping until then."

"Why must it burn?" I asked.

"We will require every snake manifestor here to get us to the Heart of the Forbidding. There will be none left to keep this place whole. And any we cannot bring with us will die in the flames."

I swallowed. "No. That can't be. There must be another way out."

He looked at me blankly and I realized that he simply didn't care. If there was another way, he hadn't bothered to look for it.

"You have five hours until we leave. If you want to find another way, you can, but if you don't sleep, you'll have nothing to give to me and it may cost us all our lives." His smile quirked in the corners and one of his eyebrows lifted. "I'm sure you'll make the wise choice, won't you, Empress? The compassionate choice?"

I cleared my throat. "What does Essa think?"

"Essa has always known her people were here for this step – to guide the Adder to the Heart of the Forbidding. Her whole life has been for this. What has your life been for?"

I swallowed. If my whole life would be spent doing this – ending the Forbidding and then ending him. Wouldn't that be worth it? After all, what you really loved, you sacrificed for. If I loved the remnants of my family – if I loved Osprey, and I did! I did! – then shouldn't I be willing to give what was left of myself for them? Was it really too much to ask?

I felt my eyes tearing up and I blinked the tears violently away. Because in my mind I saw myself sneaking kisses with Osprey and I saw myself round with his child and I saw myself playing with my nieces and nephews again, hugging my brothers and sisters. And none of that would ever happen, would it? Because even if I succeeded and I ended this, all the years of my life would be used up and I would crumple and fade and die. And so it was left to me to choose what I loved more – them or my own life.

I didn't realize Juste was still there – watching me – until I looked up and his smile turned predatory.

"Yes. I thought that would be your choice. Neither of us was made to live a boring life, Empress. We were always meant to live or die loudly and brightly. And we will. That much, I can promise you."

The darkness was a hollow, grim thing when he turned and left me there in the cold. I didn't go to seek the fires below. Instead, I huddled against the low wall of the tower in my tattered dress and cried myself to sleep.

CHAPTER FIVE

I awoke to the hum of bees. They were back. My eyes snapped open in excitement.

It was still dark, but not as dark as it would have been if a glowing golden bee hadn't popped up into my palm.

"You're back," I breathed, not sure if it was gratitude or relief that was filling me to the brim. "I've missed you, little friend. Listen to me, bee, we are in trouble."

The bee bounced on my hand as if it was trying to agree, trying to tell me something.

"I need you now more than ever. I need you to help me speak to my family. Tell them I'm going to end this. Tell them not to come for me," I whispered.

How a little bee could possibly do that – well, I didn't know. But I knew bees communicated. I knew that they spoke to one another. Maybe my bee could speak to my people for me, too.

I thought of how they could spread in a swarm. The Forbidding had claimed to have a tangle in every heart, but there was a bee for every tangle. As a swarm, there was no evil they couldn't unwind, no hurt they couldn't at least try to heal. They could do this, too. I had every confidence in them.

"You're going to have to fly very high, above the flames. And very far – all the way back to the colonies. Can you do this for me, little bee? Can you fly and fly and fly and be free like I never can again?"

The bee spun a circle around my head like a golden ring and then zipped up into the air.

"Fly with speed and blessing, little be. You hold my hope in your heart. Pollinate it across the land as you go."

As she sped away, I sent my heart with him and all my love and my last goodbyes. I'd probably never see that little bee again – just like I'd never see my loved ones again. But if I did this right, they would all be free and safe again. I just needed to focus. I just needed to be faithful. I just needed to do as I must.

I rose in the darkness, calling another bee to my palm to light my way down the spiral stairs outside the tower. My muscles were stiff and my bones ached as if I'd slept three nights instead of three hours and my torn dress was barely thick enough to keep even a brush of the cold at bay.

When I reached the fires below, I found those who came with me fast asleep under blankets and in the jackets they'd worn here. None of them had offered me anything at all. This proved that I was Empress to them only in name. But I'd known that. Just as they were my people only in name. I'd hesitated over killing Juste before. But I knew now that I'd kill him without even thinking twice about it. Because I knew what the alternative looked like. And even if I could forget watching my brother's body hanging at the end of a noose, or seeing my father slain for having the audacity to stand with me, or seeing Glorious Ingvar burn and her people lined up for the slaughter, I would still have Returning Aella's view of things and I would know how things would have looked with Juste in charge of them. And I would know that the only hope anyone had at all was that I would rise and do the only thing an Empress could ever do – take care of an Emperor.

I was clenching my jaw hard when Essa slipped in beside me. We stood together in the darkness out of earshot of the rest.

"They can't understand me. Only you and the Adder," she said. "The Adder has said he will bring his Wings – the abominations with the spirit-birds – and one of his warriors. The rest he will leave here with my people. I, alone, will go as his guide to the seat."

I turned to her and looked into her hollow eyes. "Why not bring everyone? You have snake manifestors. And they will be useful. You have many civilians here to farm and herd and tend this place."

"I can only bring six with me through the final gate," she said, her voice very certain. "And only eight with me through the first gate."

I watched her eyes for a hint of anything to explain what she was saying. Regret flashed through them so quickly that I wondered if I'd even seen it at all. And then I realized what she was saying.

"You're leaving everyone else to die," I said grimly. "The civilians. Your snake manifestors. Our Claws. Everyone but those first eight and you."

"You're only half right," she said, and this time, there was only steely determination in her eyes.

Half right. I paused, thinking, and for a moment, I was rocked by a memory from the Hissan. A memory of a man saying goodbye to everyone he loved and looking toward a dark tangled throne.

"Everyone will die," I said eventually. "Everyone here and everyone who goes with you."

"It is the price we pay," she said at last. "Judgment for our sins. Judgment for the past. A restoration that none of us will ever see. Perhaps my son … if he still lives."

"He lives," I said grimly. "As much as I wonder if that is good for anyone but you."

She shook her head. "How can you know what is best? You are an abomination. And you are already dead. The moment you walked into the flames you died. It just hasn't caught up with you yet."

"How lovely," I said to her with a steely tone. "Someone should record your words for future generations. They're so pleasant, I'm sure they'll want to remember them."

She ignored my sarcasm. "My words have been sealed and placed in the ground. When the fire has burned out and our people emerge from under the earth, they will find all I have said. They will understand."

"That you sold the living for a hope and a prophecy?" I asked, looking out at the sleeping people around the fires.

"That I did it for them. That they may once more walk under the sun. Now. Wear this cloak. It will guard you from the elements.

I tugged on the Hissan cloak – a strange piece made of sewn strips of snakeskin. I kept the sword, and the crown, and my shredded dress, but clumps of my thick hair fell free as I shrugged on the cloak. It had been singed so badly it couldn't be saved. I threw the chunks to the ground. No point getting precious about lost hair when you were going to die very soon.

"Wake the Adder and tell him the time has come," Essa said. "Then follow the stairs and meet me below. We travel."

I bit my lip as I made my way through the sleeping bodies to where my emperor husband lay. My hands twitched. They wanted to snatch my sword and neatly remove his head. I could almost feel what it would be like. It would only take a moment and a firm hand and then we'd be rid of him forever.

What was wrong with me? When had I become so twisted?

I'd been stripped down to my core and it turned out I was more wicked than I'd imagined. Maybe the voice in the tower was right. Maybe we all had a twisted bit of the Forbidding inside of us. Maybe that was all that was left inside of me.

I reached for Juste but before I touched him, his hand came out and caught my wrist. His eyes snapped open.

"Wife." His tone was danger and violence.

"Emperor," I returned. The snakes on his crown were looking at me again. "Essa says we are ready to leave. Eight people only."

"Mmmm." His eyes glittered in the light of my bee and I saw he was considering it.

He licked his lips and then he reached out lightning-fast and slid his hand under the collar of my shirt, over his feather stuck in my chest. I'd been in so much distress before that I hadn't realized how much it hurt to have him touch me there – where I'd tried to dig the feather out myself. I felt it the moment he started to steal all my power. My bee winked out, the buzzing stopped, and it felt like I hadn't slept at all. I swayed, struggling to stay upright.

"You didn't have to do that," I gasped. "You could have left me the strength to stand."

He surged to his feet and pulled me up after him. "If you haven't realized it by now, Empress, you should have. I will always take whatever can be taken. I will never stop until the world is all mine."

I didn't have the strength to shiver. He pulled me along after him until we reached Elodie. He nudged her with the toe of his boot, and she was on her feet in an instant.

"Le Majest." There wasn't even a hint of sleep in her voice.

"Attend the Empress."

She took my arm, not even asking me why I was stumbling like I was intoxicated when the rest of them were perfectly well-rested. Juste hurried to rouse Xectare, nudging her with his toe as well. She was quick to wake the other Wings and they were all quick to gather little bundles from the lone carabao cart.

They'd planned this, I realized, without the others in their party realizing it. Or maybe they did realize it and just preferred to sleep until they died.

My heart was suddenly beating twice as fast from the combination of dread and compassion. It was hard to look at those faces – softened by sleep – without feeling the urge to rouse them all and save them somehow from this. It was hard not to think of who might miss them. They were simple soldiers who had obeyed orders. They might be loving sons or husbands. They might be protective fathers and brothers. They might be good people. And they were all going to burn and I seemed to be the only one who cared.

I kept looking back at them as Juste led us away from those who slumbered to where an arched doorway led to stairs going down into the earth.

"Don't look back," Elodie growled. "Always look ahead."

Perhaps Juste should have married her. She matched him

perfectly in heartlessness and single-minded determination. And she was committed to seeing him reach his goal. I wondered if she realized she was meant to die. Juste certainly did not. He would never intentionally sacrifice himself if there was any other option. And there were always other options.

I almost gasped when we reached the bottom of the stairs to where Essa stood, calm and collected, a flaming green torch in her hand. Whatever made the flame green smelled strongly of something earthy and herbal. She held it high and behind her were three arches and a podium with a map etched on its surface. The undertrails.

"Why limit the number to nine if you're using the undertrails?" I asked tiredly. I hadn't even realized I'd asked that question out loud until Juste turned on me.

"Don't waste our guide's time with questions. If she says the route is limited to nine, it's limited to nine. If she says it will require all their power, then that is what it will require."

There was the sound of footsteps on the rocks behind us and Elodie turned to see who was there – just enough to turn me, too.

Six Hissan – men and women – surrounded us, their faces hard with resolve. Snakes poured from their hands, wrapping around each other and then joining Essa's snake.

"One last time, for the future, my friends," she said gravely. "For the oath we swore. For the Hissan."

"For the Hissan," they echoed.

And then she put her finger on the map and Elodie jerked me roughly forward. I craned my neck to get a look at the map and nearly gasped. If this map was correct – and how could it not be when the other maps were correct before? Then we were so far into the Forbidding already, but this single hop would plunge us deep into the parts of the map that were nothing but black tangles to those of us from the Winged Empire. I struggled to see more detail, but I was pulled roughly away. Why did they leave this crown on my head when I was nothing but a glorified prisoner?

"Through the middle door," Essa said. "Hurry."

"But," I started to protest. After all, these doors hadn't required anything from us before. Just faith. They hadn't needed magic and they hadn't seemed to have any limit to what they could do. Why leave everyone else here when they could go with us? "We could bring them all through these –"

I didn't have time to finish my objection. Juste nodded sharply and Elodie pulled me along with her, striding toward the middle door. She stepped through smartly, bringing me – willing or not – in step with her.

Just like the last time I'd walked into the undertrails, the trail seemed to fold me into it. Reflexively, I reached toward the skies with my heart.

Skies above, give me peace. Stars and skies and all that is above you, show me mercy. Let me spend my life for this one, last thing – the destruction of evil. Peace for my family and my land. Skies have mercy. Skies grant peace.

And, unexpectedly, like the first strawberry of summer, there was peace. The kind of peace that exists alongside sorrow. The kind that makes it possible to do the things you thought couldn't be done. I let myself sink into it as I was battered and folded and kneaded by the undertrails and the magic of the Forbidding.

It felt like it took longer this time, as if days and weeks had passed while I was taking a single step. It left me feeling hollow

– as if I had lost something I didn't know I had. Maybe what I'd lost was time.

When – at last – on shaking legs, we stumbled out the other side, I blinked into the light as if I hadn't seen light in months. Beside me, Elodie did the same.

"What was that?" she gasped and when I blinked senselessly at her, I saw that a strand of her dark hair had turned completely white.

"The undertrails," I said, croaking as if my voice hadn't been used in weeks. "Come."

I stumbled forward, knowing the others would be right behind me. My weak legs took me as far as the podium with the map. I clung to it, staring at a continent revealed more than I'd ever seen before. Beside me, Elodie collapsed on the ground, but I hung on to the podium, tracing the lines with my finger. We were so far from home it was hard to comprehend it. If I left today. If I left immediately on foot – it would take months to get home. I stared at that map blankly. I didn't even realize I was crying until the teardrops fell on the hard surface of the map, running down and pooling in the relief where the ocean was drawn. The spot where Glorious Ingvar was located must have been extra deep. My tears collected there like a map back to where this had started.

There were footsteps behind me. Moans and gasps. I would have turned to look, but I didn't have the strength. I felt like I'd been wrung out and tossed aside. I could barely keep my head up.

Someone's voice – Essa, I thought – wheezed out from behind me.

"We rest. Until we can stand, we rest."

But we hadn't rested long before Juste was urging us up again.

"Hold her tightly," he told Elodie, and then we did it again, stepping through the gate as Essa began to keen from the pressure. Her voice had risen to a scream when the trail folded us in and began to knead us again. Elodie's grip slipped from my arm and I remembered what Essa said – she could only take six through the second gate. How did she know that for sure? And was she wrong? Maybe she was so tired, she could only take four.

"Stars have mercy. Skies have mercy," I prayed until at last we stumbled from the grasp of the undertrail and stumbled again into a plain room with a podium and an open door.

Something tinkled in the distance like windchimes. From outside the yawning, open door. I stumbled toward the light and heard Essa try to protest from behind me as the others tumbled through to our final destination, but she made nothing more than a strangled moan. I didn't bother to argue. I was thirsty. And there might be water out there. Anything was better than waiting in this room with the people planning to kill me.

There were seven of us left. Just like she planned. No Claws. No Elodie with her fanatical devotion and white streak in her hair. Despite the fact she'd been nothing but my jailor, I felt a stab of misery at the thought she was gone. She'd been loyal and faithful and Juste had walked into this knowing he'd sacrifice her. I tried not to dwell on it, but her face kept coming back to mind.

I stumbled out the door and light flooded my vision so that I had to squint against it. The air felt cool. Clear of smoke. And right in front of the doorway, a fountain flowed, rising from the mouth of a curving snake statue and spewing into a pool with no hard edges. It was just stone with a slow slope that became water and then the snake. I fell to my knees beside it the pool and drank, not even wondering if the water was safe.

And when I was done, I lay down on my back and looked up at the searing sky, feeling so far from home. It made this whole journey seem surreal and unlikely and wrong. I closed my eyes, wanting to see my bees, wanting to see if they'd found Osprey or my family, and brought my last message to them. But maybe that was too soon. Maybe I hadn't spent months in the undertrails. Maybe it was just that it felt that way.

I wanted to give up right there and just sink into the ground and let it all be over. I'd been fighting too hard, for too long and now I was so, so alone. I bit my lip and let the tears come for a moment.

No, Aella, no. You can't do this. You aren't the girl who gives up. You're House Shrike and you are relentless. And you aren't done yet.

"I will not relent," I whispered. "I will not."

"Well that's good," Juste said roughly. I heard a slurp, like he was drinking water in a way that would shock his elegant self any other time. "Because we don't have time for relenting. We just left all those people to die. And you might not think that I care much about that – maybe I don't. But I do care about wasting resources and I wouldn't have wasted their lives on nothing."

He was awfully talkative for someone who looked like they'd just clawed their way out of their own grave. I blinked at him owlishly as I tried to get my thoughts in order. He was crouched beside me, slurping water from a cupped hand. His face had long, red scratches on either cheek – like he'd gripped his own face and torn into the flesh with his nails. His eyes were dark holes, ringed in purple, and his perfect hair was in disarray, his perfect clothing hanging half-on and half-off. He looked like he'd survived a hurricane. And given how the undertrails tended to … intensify … a person, maybe he had.

I struggled back up to my feet while he struggled to his.

"What now?" I asked. "Is the Heart of the Forbidding here?"

"The test is here, somewhere," he said and I wondered if he was even talking to me, though to my shock he took my hand in his. I tried to jerk my hand away, but his grip was surprisingly vice-like. He sounded almost as if he was in a trance as he pulled me after him. "We've been together through all of this, Empress. From the moment I took my destiny in both hands and seized the manifestation of my magic, you've been there. You stood with me when I was weighed and measured in the temple."

That was a convenient way to remember it. I had been the one tested while he was the one who watched. Just thinking of it rocked me with a sudden Hissan memory. For a fleeting moment I watched an artist carving the face of this snake fountain, chisel in hand, face screwed up in concentration while a cluster of well-dressed Hissan spoke off to one side. "It will be here to greet the Adder one day. Before his final trials. Make it worthy."

I shook my head, feeling like there was more to all of this than I had the ability to grasp.

"Yes, you've been there with me. It's fitting that you be with me now, as it all comes together," Juste was saying and whether he was just now telling himself this wild story, or whether he'd always been telling it to himself, I couldn't tell. "I did everything I could to prepare you. From offering my own brother to cleanse you in the river and keep you safe in your travels, to making you indispensable to our allies. To crowning you Empress beside me. We've been a team together this whole time."

He was mad. Utterly, raving mad.

"We're following my vision for a nation of love and peace. We will prove ourselves to all the world for who we truly are – people deeply motivated by tolerance and freedom."

That left me as the only sane person here because everyone else was following his mad lead. He said words like 'tolerance' and 'love' but his actions proved he had no idea what they meant.

"And now we face our last trial," he said as he drew me around the snake fountain and I suddenly realized why all I'd been seeing was sky.

We were up on a high rise of land where the snake fountain was the pinnacle and as Juste led me around it, we could look out over a long field before us.

I gasped.

Everything was so very bright in the noon sun that it was hard for me to see anything at all, but what I did see was a long field of rank upon rank of men and women in Hissan uniform, armed with polearms and long thin shields. When they caught sight of Juste they made a complicated "S" sign of salute and stomped their feet in a way that made the whole valley ring.

My heart leapt into my throat. From one army to another. From one source of insanity to another. It was like Juste was carried on wings of eagles from height to height with never a moment where he had to pay for the lives he spent or the deaths he accumulated.

Behind the army, was another rise and at the top of that rise was some kind of dark tangle. All around the valley, the forbidding reached for that tangle like spokes of a wheel. And my heart was beating so hard at the sight of them that I thought it might burst. The spokes were moving – twisting and reaching like chained dogs all desperate for the same bone just out of their grasp. They were spaced at regular intervals through this valley, all except for one – the road right before us that split through the waiting armies. That was a wheel spoke, too, but unlike the clawing, reaching tentacles, this one was frozen. It still looped and whorled, but it stayed utterly still. I tried to trace it with my gaze, but it defied inspection. Somehow, it was like the spirit world was twisted with the physical in such a way that the physical only met our reality here and there and everywhere else it ducked and wove and tangled.

"The last test."

The voice behind me startled me. It was Essa. She was swaying, biting her lip hard as if that was the only thing keeping her on her feet. Blood poured down her chin.

She spoke louder now, her voice thundering over the people assembled in the valley below.

"Behold, I bring to you the Adder on the Day marked by prophecy, at the Time foretold. And with him come the Companions as it has been written."

It felt so fitting that I wasn't at all surprised when my memory flashed to a time before and another time and another – one Hissan memory layered over the next and embedded into me by the snake. They were the memories of the Hissan telling their children of the prophecy and repeating it on holy days. And telling it to one another in times of crisis and under all that a memory of a woman slick with sweat, clutching a wound in her belly as she gave the very first of the prophecies.

But why did this memory wait until now to surface?

Her words answered my question.

"For behold," she gasped in my memory. "The time will come that the Adder will step out on the Plains of the Wheel to find the Seat of the Adder. And the Time will be Noon on the

Day one full moon cycle after the Flames have died across the Forbidding. And the Cycle of the rising and growth of judgment will come to an end for the Final judgment shall come. The Adder will strike his foot on our rocks and with him will come abominations of Wings. And all will fall but one, for the healing of our land, the return of our blood, the righting of wrongs done unto us. And on that day, the people will accept the judgment and will end all wars for the renewal of the land and the rebirth of the stones and rocks of it and the deep tangle of judgment, the dark tentacles of retribution will finally return to the heart of the earth and peace shall reign and the dead will return. But only after those who come are sifted and tested and the blood has been spilled and the sickness drawn out and the healing begun."

And then her eyes glazed over, and death took her.

I drew a long, shuddering breath, and I knew this was the only way. I would die here. And so would the other Wings. And Juste would end this. But if I died here, who would end Juste?

I bit my lip, and the taste of my blood reminded me that it wasn't over yet.

I turned to Juste and in a low voice that I hoped did not show how much I craved vengeance, I said, "It is time to be sifted, husband."

CHAPTER SIX

If the Hissan were like the Winged Empire, they would have fed us something more than a few handfuls of dates and dried meat and a hurried skin of water. They would have given us the rest of the evening to rest and get ready to leave – even if they hated us – because they would have wanted us to succeed. They might have even given us mounts to take through the trial.

They expected that we were going to march down that odd, twisting tentacle and that we would save their land, and instead of honoring us, they acted like we'd shown up late and tracked mud all over their floors. Which was very Hissan. If a prophecy said a thing, they expected it done regardless of what the person doing it might think. We were only tools to them. Good or evil, loved or unloved outside this place and time – none of that meant anything to them.

In a contest for who I hated more – the Hissan or the Winged Empire, the Winged Empire would always win, but the Hissan were trying very hard to catch up.

A man with two snakes winding around his arms and a neck as thick as my thigh strode forward as we were being hurriedly fed and Essa was trying to explain how she'd brought us here.

"Honor to you, Essa," he said as he approached, and she bowed very low. She had to be helped to straighten she was so exhausted. He ignored her weakness, not offering any assistance as he continued. "The last help to the offerings will be your honor to give."

She nodded and she seemed more resigned than excited. Were they just as callous with their own people as they were with us?

He turned to us, rubbing his bald head with one hand. "I am Fierze, Lord of Asps, Radiant over the Crystal Caverns and as the highest of the Hissan nation, I welcome you to the testing. May prophecy prevail. May your blood purge this land."

Behind him, his troops clashed their polearms against their narrow shields to echo his words. I squinted my eyes trying to see beyond them, but there was no camp here. There were no tents. Had they really come for this one moment, trusting prophecy so much that they would make the journey to arrive for a specific time with no guarantee that it would come to pass?

"May your blood pay the price!" He bellowed loudly and the troops cheered his words. It made my head ring. I was still dizzy from the undertrails and all this noise was not helping.

The way he said blood made my stomach twist as if he was looking forward to seeing us dead. Which he was, wasn't he? That was why they didn't waste food on us beyond what they must. That was why they simply watched us with cold eyes as they prepared to put us to their test. That was why they called us 'the offering.' It made my skin crawl and I tried not to consciously scratch at it.

"None of us knows how you will be tested, only that it must be done. The Adder must be tested with the heretics who come to this place on this day by his side."

That was me and the other Wings. How charming. Heretics. If I wasn't already committed to this path, that kind of attitude would make me want to do my best to sabotage it. I glanced furtively at the Wings, wondering if they felt the same, but their faces were cold masks like Juste's. Their eyes held the same disdain his held. I could almost feel the message they were giving off with their body language – we are above this. Babble all you like, barbarians. We have come for our own reasons and purposes and you are nothing but a delay.

"You are to be our witnesses, then?" Juste asked, looking around. His arrogance seemed utterly unaffected by them. Perhaps he'd grown used to people wanting him dead. His father had left him vying for his life with Osprey. Osprey would kill him in a heartbeat if he'd ever had the chance to do it without seeing someone else hurt because of it. And I was his wife and I desperately wanted him dead. Was there anyone in his life who didn't?

"I will stand vigil for you when you enter," the Lord of Asps said. "I, and I alone will wait to see if you succeed or the darkness takes you. As it was spoken, so it will be done. The Adder and the heretics will enter the test. The Watcher will remain for a year and a day to see the task is completed."

Two Hissan walked out from behind him, their faces unnaturally pale and greenish-tinged. There was one male and one female, their hair long and black, their hands filled with the twisting coils of their spirit-snakes. They said nothing to us and did not acknowledge us in any way. They simply stood behind their leader, muttering together.

Everyone was just acting like this was entirely usual – that an army would wait to see a bunch of foreigners arrive and then they would stick them into a trial that should probably kill them and just leave so they could get home in time for dinner. How lovely. If I wasn't already certain that all this was leading to my death, I would be now.

I didn't want to die. But I saw no other options. I just needed to keep my head from spinning enough to make sure that Juste died with me. That was all. If I could focus on that, I could make my heart stop racing, my hands stop sweating and my mouth stop going so dry. Right?

It was a battle to control my body. It wanted to run. Or vomit. Or do anything to push all this away from me.

"I and only I will bear witness to this great act," the Lord of Asps said smoothly.

"And the army will leave?" I asked because I needed to say something to distract myself from thinking. Thinking was making me panic.

The Lord of Asps eyes my crown, his eyes narrowing to slits. Oh yes, birds. They didn't like birds.

"It could take you a full turning of seasons," Essa whispered from behind me. "Time passes within the test as it does in the undertrails, as it does in the Forbidding, as it does in all the places touched by the judgment."

"Three months?" I asked, aghast.

"No, not a change of seasons," she scolded. "A turning of seasons."

I paused. "A year."

She nodded.

"You're going to wait here a full year for us?"

She looked away.

"This servant, Essa, will not stand vigil. Her blood will pay your passage as is her honor for finding the Adder and bringing him here in fulfillment of prophecy," Fierze said grimly.

I looked directly into his eyes. She'd done what they needed, and they were going to kill her. She wasn't going to get out alive, either. Not even after all her friends had to die. Not even now when these other snake manifestors could help here so she didn't have to do this alone.

I shook my head in judgment. "And what will happen to your people and your prophecies when all this is over?"

I tried to keep the snap out of my voice, but I couldn't help it.

"Peace," The Lord of Asps spoke with the firmness of a ruling. His lips firmed as he pressed them together. He was treating me as if I was a fussy child he was setting down. "An end to war. The death of a few for such a great goal is not to be mourned but celebrated."

I shook my head again, crossing my arms over my chest. I felt nothing but condemnation for these people. Was there nowhere I could go where the people weren't like this? Everywhere was the same. A few people who thought they were elite and above it all spent the lives, and treasure, and hopes of those under them on their wild bids for more power, more renown, more wealth. If the Forbidding truly was the land rising against them, then I didn't blame it at all. What kind of peace would it be if it cost them nothing? How long would it last? Would it just be until they could maneuver for more power and more people to oppress?

"And when I have completed this task," Juste said coolly. "I shall ascend to your throne and your armies and lands shall be mine – as it is written."

The prophecy hadn't said anything about that. I noticed – barely – that Fierze glanced at him and then at Essa who spoke with such smooth subtlety that I would never have guessed her comment had anything to do with Juste's if I hadn't heard the prophecy myself.

"Due to circumstances beyond the control of the Adder, he had to offer up a substitute in the temple," she smiled faintly. "My son, Ixtap, took it upon himself to give to the Adder what wisdom was deemed necessary."

Fierze smiled and nodded but it looked wooden, like he was thinking very furiously behind that cold face of his. They'd expected the Adder to be prepared. For what? I didn't feel prepared for anything and I was the one with all the memories.

"We should begin," Juste said, striding toward the tangle of Forbidding that was the frozen spoke of the wheel. He wasn't watching Essa. But I was, and I saw her subtle nod to me and the slight raising of Fierze's eyebrows.

They didn't want to tell Juste that he was meant to die. That "blood" didn't mean his noble birth. "Blood" was meant literally – his blood splashed over their rocks. His blood dripping through the holes on the Seat of the Adder. I supposed they didn't care how they got their willing sacrifice, only that they got him. And I didn't want to tell him, either, because if they had to kill him to get the blood they wanted, that could only be a good thing for me.

But I was chewing my lip because I just didn't know. I didn't trust these people. I didn't trust their random prophecies or the weird memories they'd put in my head. All of this felt like some kind of bizarre nightmare I should be able to wake up from.

Essa hurried to get ahead of Juste, guiding him to the correct spot along the tangle of Forbidding. It all looked the same to me, but something must have told her where to go. There was a nervousness in her movements. And no wonder. She was spending the last moments of her life arranging details for other people. There was no honor in this. It wasn't right.

I didn't even notice that Fierze had fallen into stride with me.

"And so, you are the one who holds our memories."

"Yes," I agreed. The other Wings were between me and Juste, looking around them with hard eyes and pursed lips. How was Juste keeping them with us? They looked like they might flee at any minute.

"Then you will know when the time comes and what you must do and I can only hope you will choose wisely," he said, never even looking at me.

"It's not your life on the line," I hissed. "You don't have to pay any price at all."

"What price would you have me pay?" he asked, acid in his voice.

"Real peace," I said. "Peace with my people on the shores of the ocean."

"The peace you are buying is peace with the Forbidding," he said dismissively.

Ahead of us, Essa stopped beside the wheel spoke of frozen Forbidding, closed her eyes, and let her snake slip through her fingers. It reared back and then struck the tangle, its fangs digging into the dark magic. There was a sound like a crack and then a real crack appeared, and the snake shoved itself into the gap, glowing a bright green as it widened that crack further and further. She began to shake as if she had run a long way and her body were failing. I didn't want to watch her, and yet I couldn't look away. How much must she want this that she was willing to give her life for a single part of it?

"Then I guess you can wait out here and hope I do what you want," I hissed to the Lord of Asps, my eyes glued on Essa. "Hope that I care about your people the way you clearly don't care about mine."

I risked a glance at him. He looked shaken for a moment, but he still hadn't looked at me.

I was rocked suddenly by a vision and I gasped. Osprey's face swam into view with a look of such devastated hope that it nearly broke my heart.

"You live," he whispered to my bee. "You live. We all thought you had perished in the flames with Le Majest."

My bee shuddered and his face flickered. I felt like maybe – somehow – the bee was passing on his message to Osprey – that I loved my family. That I would die for them. Not to rescue me.

"Hold on, House Apidae," he said, his voice urgent. "I will come for you."

I blinked and the vision was gone.

Bring it back! Bring it back!

Everything in me felt like it was wrenching apart as my mind strained to return to the bee. But my connection was lost.

There was only one place I wanted to be – only one person I wanted to be near – and I'd never have that again. If only I'd had a few more seconds before it was gone. I fought a wave of sadness, blinking back my tears.

"The time has come," Essa announced loudly. "The price will be paid."

Juste whispered something and Wing Xectare's face went stone cold and firm and then she stepped through the spirit snake's body and into the gap.

Essa let out a wail, clutching her chest with her arms and bending at the waist. Her face twisted with pain … and was that regret? I felt a surge of sympathy slice through me, leaving me wanting to sob with her.

Wing Essena was next and now Essa fell to her knees keening in what sounded like agony. She was dying right here before us and no one so much as looked at her. My eyes smarted and my vision blurred with unshed tears.

No death should be treated casually. No one was expendable. Not Elodie. Not Essa. No one.

Fury bubbled up within me. And for just a moment, I felt the hum of my bees returning. Our rage flowed hot and fast. This was wrong. We would rise against it. We would …

I'd taken two strides when Fierze grabbed my arm and halted me. I spun, the fury I felt making my face hard.

"Succeed and you will have bought your peace," he said grimly his eyes widening at what he saw in my face. I realized that while I had been seeing the vision of Osprey and watching Essa, he'd been considering my threat. "Succeed and you win."

"And I die," I said quietly, shaking with my rage.

"It's part of the price. Essa is paying hers. Pay your price and your people will see peace." He was looking into my eyes now – and he looked honest, but how could I tell? There was no way to hold a stranger to a promise. But this was probably the best I was going to get. I nodded firmly and he released my arm and let me follow the rest into the arm of the Forbidding.

My vision flickered and I saw Osprey's face, saw that he was looking down into a cupped hand.

"Hold on little bee. Hold on for her."

He vanished again and I felt like something had been torn from my chest.

Juste was waiting for me and as I stepped forward, he caught my eye.

"This is what I made you Empress for," he said urgently. "This is why we were chosen."

But I wasn't insane like him. I knew enough to be terrified.

My vision filled with Osprey again and I froze, trying to drink in a last look at him.

"Wherever you go, my honeybee, I will find you. If you travel to the ends of the earth, I will seek you out. If they drag you to the depths of the earth or under the sea, even that will not be too far for me. Take heart. I'm coming."

I blinked back tears as a hand clamped around my arm, dragging me into the gap in the wall of Forbidding. Beside us, Essa's wail turned into a death rattle. The moment my feet touched the gap, the vision of Osprey popped like a soap bubble and I knew somehow that it wasn't coming back this time.

CHAPTER SEVEN

"Well, this is odd," Xectare said in a chilly voice from somewhere ahead of me.

Everything was pitch black. I could see nothing at all. I would not give in to fear. I would not let death decide who I would be while I still lived.

A cold hand caught my arm and tugged me another step forward and I surged into the light. Xectare had a hand raised with her swan poised above it, wings expanded and milky light flooding over us. Her expression was tense and her eyes flitted around the room like butterflies in a garden.

We appeared to be in a room of some kind made entirely by tangled black tentacles from roof to ceiling. I had the worst feeling that I was inside something's guts. I shuddered at the thought.

There was no exit or entrance that I could see. No window or gap. No place for a fire or water or anything that might be of comfort and I had a cold certainty in my belly that comfort was not a priority for whoever – whatever – had built this place. There was a chair.

Black and imposing with slashes carved through the seat and seat back, made from tangles of Forbidding with a high back and ornamentation, it stood on a small, raised dais. It didn't look like something made by men. It looked like something that had grown there – like a tree mishappen or a strange rock. As if something that had no concept of sitting had tried to make a chair. Even odder, there was a tall, round table in front of it and it was ringed with smaller high-backed chairs, like imitations of the first one.

We moved toward it by instinct.

"The Seat of the Adder," Juste gasped almost reverently.

I felt the floor ripple under my feet – not enough to move me, just enough to remind me that it was alive. I'd never missed the feeling of rock underfoot with such fervency before. If I had to die, I wished it could have been out in the open on still, mindless rock instead of in the belly of the Forbidding.

Juste was stalking toward the seat, eyes lit and face in awe. He pulled me after him and I let him. There was nowhere else to go but here and no point in fighting it.

"You promised us names, Emperor. I want to hear that confirmed again," Essena said in a trembling voice.

"Fight this battle with me and you will have your name, Swan" Juste said absently.

He brought me right up to the table before he let go of my hand so he could run his over the curving ornamentation of the chair. He seemed to be holding his breath as he examined it, as if this was a thing he was longing for rather than a terrible gamble. And then he sat in the Seat as easily as if he was sitting in the Winged Palace in Kestrel City and he let out a long breath.

I took the seat next to him. Being beside him was no worse than being beside any of these people. They were all snakes. They just weren't as honest about that as Juste was.

"You will all have your names," he said when he had calmed

down. “Owl. Raven. Eagle. And whichever of you proves the most useful to me in this, you will replace Wing Osprey at my right hand.”

Everyone had manifested by the time they took their seats. Even me. My single bee sat gently on the back of my hand. I clung to his hum – the only friendly thing in this dark place.

I didn’t want to look at the mushroom-like tangle of the table. I didn’t want to look at the pulsing walls. I just wanted to think of my bee.

Be with me until the end, if you can, I pled in my mind to my fuzzy friend. I didn’t want to say the words out loud and let my enemy know what was happening inside my heart. Stay with me, little bee. I need you.

The rest of them seemed satisfied with Juste’s words. Almost smug.

Was the space around us getting smaller or was it was just my imagination? Between that and the subtle movement, I had the worst feeling of being swallowed up. It made me feel like I might vomit. I was even starting to sweat. I rubbed my forehead with the back of my hand and tried to concentrate.

The table was etched with a map – not just of Far Stones. I saw the Winged Empire on it, too, and the island chains of Garbocco, Rajadeer, Haberno, Javens, and other nations I’d hardly bothered to note in the past. They weren’t labeled, but little glowing points showed on the map on the continent of the Winged Empire and on the continent of the Far Stones. They glowed different colors.

“A game?” the eagle manifestor asked. He was picking at something on his cheek – a burn scab, I realized from our time in the Forbidding – and his eyes were fixed through their glass panels on the map. "How is that a test?"

"None of this makes sense," Essena said. "The Hissan say that the Forbidding is judgment come to life. And yet they make towers out of the stuff and underground passages that instantly transport you halfway across the map. Why involve yourself with something you see as a threat?"

Why indeed. I examined the map, keeping my face still.

"Then perhaps they made this place as well," Wing Xectare suggested. She was very calm in her manner, spreading her fingers across the table just outside the ring of the circular map, her eyes narrowing as she studied it. Her pale white hair rippled slightly. Was there a breeze? I couldn't feel it. "After all, they prophesied that the Adder would come here so perhaps they set this test up for him. They couldn't have known it would be our Emperor."

I didn't think so. This felt nothing like how the Hissan operated. If they wanted to test us, they'd torture us with their snakes like what they'd done to me in the temple.

CLEVER GIRL.

I shuddered at the sound of the Forbidding's voice in my mind. No one else so much as flinched. Did they not hear it, or did it not bother them like it bothered me?

THE SSSNAKE IS ENDLESSSS. ALL HEARTSS WILL BE OURSSS. THERE'S A LITTLE OF OUR TANGLE IN EVERY ONE OF YOU.

There was a little in my heart. That's why Juste could control me.

Part of me was watching as the Wings studied the map, their birds moving to hover over each of them. Juste manifested his snake, letting it come out and tangle around his body. It would have been a scene fit for a painter if it wasn't so spooky.

WE SSSEE YOUR POSSSIBILITIES. YOUR ITERATIONSSS. YOU COULD BE THIS GIRL. OR ANOTHER. OR ANOTHER. WE KNEAD. WE FOLD. WE FIND THE REAL YOU. EVIL MUST BE EXPOSED TO BE JUDGED. THE HEART MUST BE SUNDERED TO BE WEIGHED.

Because that wasn't at all creepy.

THIS TEST WILL FIND YOUR ITERATIONS.

Without meaning to, my mind flicked back to traveling through the fire, to watching my other shadow selves when different choices were made – to watching them die or suffer. Those were iterations of me. Hadn't the Forbidding already weighed me?

DEEP IN THE DARK, DOWN IN THE STONE,

FOLLOW THE EARTHBEAT AND FIND MY HOME.

I remembered that poem. And that's where it had taken us now – deep into the dark. Were we being moved even now down into the stone? I concentrated and it was likely my imagination, but I could almost sense a heartbeat coming up through my feet – subtle, barely there, and yet I could sense it.

But last time I heard that poem when I spoke to the Forbidding in the tower, it had said something about not being able to untangle what was tangled.

NOT WITHOUT BLOOD. NOT WITHOUT SSSACRIFICE.

What did it want from us?

EVERYTHING.

What would it do when it had it?

LIVE.

I shuddered again.

What was it?

WE TOLD YOU. WE ARE JUDGMENT COME ALIVE. WE ARE ALL THE THINGS YOU DENIED TAKING ROOT AND FLOURISHING. WE WILL SEE OUR REVENGE.

"Empress? Empress." Pain brought me back to what was in front of me and my hand flew up to cup my aching cheek.

"You slapped me," I gasped. But why was I surprised? Slapping me was hardly the worst thing Juste had done to me.

"Tell me that vision was useful," he hissed. "Tell me you learned something."

"The Forbidding wants us dead so it can live," I said.

Wing Essena rolled her eyes. "The opinion of the Empress is not worthy of you, Emperor. Her only use is as a well of power for you to drain."

"Mmm." He didn't deny it, but he was watching me with a weighing look in his eyes. "Not yet. We will wait and see what is required before I decide what to do with her energy."

Essena's eyes lit as if she thought he was going to give some of my energy to her. Could he even do that? I wasn't worried. Juste was too selfish to share. It was his nature. As if to punctuate that thought, his snake shifted around him, rolling up his arm to look straight into my eyes.

"What do you think, Wing Jann?" Juste asked the woman with the golden raven. She was biting her bottom lip, considering the map. "What is this game?"

"It's high stakes," she said. "The Hissan made that clear. I don't think they knew what it was beyond that."

Or beyond the fact that we might be trapped here for a year. I looked around me nervously. With nothing to eat or drink except what the others brought in their small bundles, we wouldn't last this place for very long. Could we even survive through the test?

"The only way to know for sure, Le Majest," Wing Xectare said. "Is to try it. Might I suggest that you ask your Empress to sit it out until we are certain? I can see the benefit she can be for you, but we should not forget that at heart, she is a traitor. She is only here to be of use to you."

"I forget nothing," Juste said. "One of you, be bold. Touch the map and let us see what happens next."

He reached out and grabbed my wrist. Maybe he hadn't acknowledged Xectare, but he was still nervous about me. Which was funny. What did they think I was going to do? I was one person, far from the centers of power, far from influence of any kind. There was nothing for me here. Not now.

And yet they were all watching me as if I was the snake here.

He met my questioning eyes.

"Wait," his eyes seemed to glitter as his gaze raked my face. His snake wrapped itself lovingly around his forehead like a second crown. "Your turn will come, Empress."

Essena's face was bold as she reached toward the table and touched a dot close to where Glorious Ingvar ought to be on the map. She froze like that. Finger in place, lips parted. And for a moment I thought she was having some kind of fit, but then her bird winked out and still she was frozen.

"Did it kill her?" the Eagle manifestor asked, his voice a whisper of horror.

The shadows around us seemed to grow with Essena's bird gone. The remaining manifestations flickered wildly with their manifestor's nervousness.

Xectare leaned in close, examining the woman who was her friend. "No. I think she is … elsewhere. For now, at least."

"Should we wait?" the Eagle manifestor asked. "Will she come back."

Juste made a disgusted sound in the back of his throat.

I wasn't paying attention to his nerves – I was trying to keep my own from taking hold of me. Breathe, Aella, breathe. You came here to die. Don't falter now. But so much of me wanted to find another way – a way to win and still live.

A way not to play this game. None of the Forbidding's games were nice. None of them left you unscarred.

"There's no way to tell what will happen," Xectare said smoothly. "None of us have done this before, either."

"Can more than one of us do this – whatever it is – at once?" the eagle pressed.

"Why don't you try and see?" Juste asked acidly. His knee was bouncing, and he kept looking around the room like a door might appear.

"Maybe we all have to do it," the Eagle manifestor said, looking worriedly from one face to another. "Or maybe it will kill the second person to try."

"Or maybe, I will kill you for cowardice," Juste's voice was low and threatening.

The Eagle manifestor licked his lips. "Maybe you could have the Empress touch it next, Emperor? Then we'll know if it's safe."

Juste laughed. "Do indulge him, Empress."

It was a drawled command, but I knew Juste well enough now to hear the steel in his words. Do it, or die.

I bit the inside of my cheek where no one could see it and slowly reached for the map. At the last second, Juste grabbed my hand and put my finger on Karkatua. The moment I touched the map there, I froze. And then my vision winked out and I had that terrible sensation of being swallowed – like the feeling of going through the undertrails but amplified by a hundred. The memory of Retger speaking to me in his room at the inn melded suddenly with the memory of Osprey holding my head underwater and then, while I thought I was still sputtering, I heard voices.

CHAPTER EIGHT

That was Zayana's voice! I could hear it.

"Zayana!" I called but I couldn't hear my own voice. It was as if I were in a dream. I couldn't see her either, just hear her voice as if I was listening through a door.

My breath caught in my throat. How was this possible?

"It could be better, Retger Shrike, that's what I'm telling you. The Winged Empire isn't lost. It's just ruled by tyrants. That's what Aella taught me – but that's not all she taught me because I watched her and I watched you and I know that you don't have to be evil, or broken, or fully submitted just because you grew up in the Winged Empire. We can be more. I know that now. I saw a red bird sitting on the limb of a tree today and underneath the tree, a frog leapt, and a beetle climbed up the bark. Surely you know what that means."

My brother's laugh held as much affection as it did derision. "Tell me what it means, tangle of my heart."

She sighed affectionately. "It means that peace is possible. A world where the Winged Empire doesn't destroy other people and nations is possible. We could choose to sit in the branch and not eat the beetle or the frog."

"It's not 'we' anymore, Zayana. It's them. And it will be them until this civil war is over."

"And when will that be?" her voice sounded tired. "If everything we've heard is true, Retger, then your sister has been crowned Empress. And she might rule someday. It could be us instead of us and them. It could be a chance for her to bring back order and make the Empire right again. Follow the signs. Right the wrongs."

My vision was starting to clear. I squinted, trying to make out as much as I could.

They were standing in a corner of a large room, their heads close together, and he was gently holding her arm in a way that suggested intimacy rather than domination. Little groups of people were clustered all across the room, talking quietly. They had the same look of weariness on their faces. Some were doing tallies, others sorting small slips of paper. I caught sight of Victore pouring over a map.

It was a planning room for the Single Wing. My heart leapt in my chest. They were still fighting. They must be still winning – and seeing Victore here meant that Raquella might still be alive. I wanted to scream with excitement. There was hope for my family. If I could just hold on.

"Retger, it's me," I said, hurrying to him, but he didn't look at me. "Retger!"

They still couldn't hear me.

"I don't want to think of my sister and that … creature," Retger growled.

Zayana looked around furtively as if even now she didn't dare be caught saying his name aloud. "I hate Juste Montpetit, too, Retger. I want him gone. And if we get our wish, then who reigns? Aella."

If only she knew how useless this talk was. I wouldn't survive Juste. Both of us were dead people walking.

"I still believe more is possible," Zayana whispered. "I believe the Empire can be saved. And that we can help with that."

I look down at my hands and gasped. I was translucent, like I wasn't here. Unable to be heard or seen. I poked the curtain beside me, and it rippled in response. I could touch. But what good would that do me?

Was this one of the Forbidding's iterations? A little game of, "what would it be like if you were a ghost?"

I wasn't impressed. I wasn't going to play this game. I took a breath and looked around the room. No, I couldn't waste this chance just because I was feeling a moment of pique.

I could be useful. There were still things I could share. I hurried over to Victore and his map.

There was a pen there and parchment. Victore had been sketching little pictures of sieges and making notes in the margins.

What wouldn't they know that I could tell them?

Hurriedly I scribbled on the page,

Civil War on main continent of Winged Empire.

Ixtap of the Hissan (original people who live in Far Stones) has led the charge to raise Juste Montpetit to the throne there using intimidation tactics.

Houses have arrayed against him. Including House Cardinal.

General Petren has fled the continent.

I wasn't sure what else to write. I paused and in that split-second moment, I saw Victore's eyes grow huge. Could he see me?

"Bees," he said with wonder in his voice. "I remember bees."

One of my bees was standing on his parchment, buzzing faintly. I reached out to grab it and it darted away.

And then the sense of being swallowed rushed over me again and the world went black. I tried not to vomit as the feeling of a throat pulsing around me and pulling me down shuddered through me.

My eyes popped open and I sagged with relief. Inside me, tension still twanged like a string plucked on a harp. My family was alive and fighting. They had Victore. All was not lost.

"What did you see?" Juste asked me.

"My brother Retger and Zayana," I said. I was too shaken to even think about lying about that. "They were arguing about whether the Winged Empire could be saved from itself."

Juste grunted. "And that was all."

This time I had the sense to choose what I would say. "They couldn't hear me or see me. I kept trying to talk to them and then I came back here."

"Hmm."

I swallowed, trying to clear the nausea from my spinning head. Hope was a heady thing. I could almost live just on that. They were alive. They were still fighting.

"What did the Eagle see?" I asked, trying to divert attention from myself.

I was surprised when he answered himself. His voice sounded rusty.

"I saw a friend, too. A man who claimed civil war has broken out on the mainland."

"Could you speak to him?" Juste asked. He must have just returned as well. The Eagle shook his head and then turned green and let his head fall into his hands.

"They came back alive," Juste said after thinking for a minute, his eyes moving from one Wing to the next as he made his decision. "And we need all the information we can get to figure out if this is a puzzle to solve. We will each try it. Prepare yourselves."

He looked around the table, meeting the eyes of each of the Wings surrounding it, and then, with great deliberateness, he chose Glorious Ingvar and set his finger on the map.

My breath hitched in my throat when Xectare set her finger on Portua Town. The Raven chose a place on the map near Kestrel City and Essena chose Glorious Ingvar, too. Interesting. What would she want with that place? Or was she merely following Juste's lead.

They all froze over the map and I met the eyes of the Eagle. My knee was bouncing. Excitement filled me up, buzzing like a swarm of bees. If this was the test, it was one I wanted. Seeing my family – even in glimpses – was more than I could have hoped for.

"Hello, Empress," he said, licking his lips nervously. "I'm not lying."

"I know," I replied, and his eyebrows rose. "Civil war has broken out on the mainland. And it will continue to rage until one side wins, or the Emperor returns to the Winged Empire. This little foray we're on will cost something."

"What will it cost?" he asked, swallowing. There was fear in his eyes.

"Time. Lives. Maybe everything," I said softly. "Tell me, Eagle. What is it that you want? What made you come to this terrible place?"

He swallowed again, but this time his eyes hardened as he spoke. "You think I'm some kind of traitor and you can expose me. But I'm not. I'm loyal to the Empire. I will be named Eagle. And when that day comes even you will fear me, you fraud of an Empress."

I raised an eyebrow, feeling the blood rush to my cheeks. He was no friend of mine. Here for pure ambition alone. But ambition was something I could work with. It could be turned. It could be channeled. I felt the blood pounding in my skull. We were here. We were this far. How could I turn all of this to my advantage – to the advantage of Far Stones? There had to be a way.

My vision blurred and I looked through my bee's eyes for just a moment to see Osprey's blue eyes on me. He smiled hopefully, sorrow thick in his eyes.

"I hope you can see me. I've been trying to find you." He looked over his shoulder nervously. "But things on the ground have changed and it will have to wait. Hold on for me. Be strong. I will find you."

He was gone before I could start to cry. I didn't know if I should despair that he would waste himself looking for me or feel hope. I shouldn't feel hope. It would only disappoint me. I was too far away for even my great hunter to find me. So why did it make me feel so warm inside to know he was still thinking of me?

Juste blinked awake again first.

"Extraordinary," he said, not noticing the byplay that had gone on in his absence. "We can affect the world even if we can't speak."

"Can we?" I asked, allowing my eyes to widen and trying to look innocent.

"Oh yes," Juste said, biting his lip thoughtfully. He shifted in his seat as if he was considering something. "Next time, wife, try writing a note. And when you do, be sure it is to remind people that I and I alone am the ultimate ruler of the Winged Empire. I will not tolerate rebellion. I will not be usurped."

He opened his mouth to say more but now the others were unfreezing.

"Report," Juste demanded.

Xectare swallowed, her face a pale green. But her words were crisp. "I saw my apprentices in the inn in Portua Town. I left a note for them, explaining that they must return home."

Juste nodded but my eyes narrowed as I watched Xectare. That seemed mild enough, but I had been one of her apprentices, so I knew she cared very little about them. But she'd clearly chosen their town for her visit. What was she hiding from us?

"I had no chance to act," the one who was called Raven said. "I found myself on a rowboat between a ship and the sea. No one could see or hear me and there was no way to leave a message of any kind."

"A pity," Juste said, staring at her as if trying to work out if this was the truth. My memory snapped back to what the voice of the

Forbidding had said – about how there was a tangle of that dark magic in each of us. I wondered if exposing our hearts like this was only the beginning – perhaps, just as we were learning it and how it worked, it was learning us.

And none of my fellow travelers trusted one another. None of them was willing to tell the whole story.

"I happened to be where a contact of mine for a previous time was laboring. I hoped to see him again so I may make inroads into that trust once more," Essena offered. She was watching Juste with the same weighing look that he was giving her.

A memory flickered into my mind – the poem from the door of the tower in Glorious Ingvar.

We keep what we catch.

Stories and souls.

Dreams and Sight.

What did the Forbidding take from us and keep?

GOOD QUESTION. BUT WILL YOU DISCOVER THE ANSWER IN TIME?

A chill shot through me. I lifted my head and studied the others one, by one. Was any of them different?

The Raven blinked, staring at a place just over Juste's shoulder as he spoke.

"It's a game," he said. "We need to maneuver our pieces into place to defeat the rebels and show we can win. Then the Forbidding will open to us. I think that's what the test is. It wants to see that we are brave and capable – worthy of power and glory. What other test would there be for rulers and gods among men?"

Maybe it just wanted to see what it could take.

But Juste seemed utterly certain. And I was just as certain that he was wrong. The Hissan had known we would die here one by one. The Forbidding didn't give rewards. It only took and took and took. It claimed it would expose our hearts. Is that what it caught just now? A sense of who we were and what we wanted? Would it test us now against that standard? Against our own dreams? Against our own sight?

I bit my lip. I would have to go in there again. And I didn't think I could fight whatever test the Forbidding was running. I could only play it as best as I could and hope to foil the efforts of the rest of those around me.

"We go in again," Juste said. "And this time, do anything you can to try to help the Wined Empire eradicate the rebel settlers known as the Single Wing. Anything you can. Be sure to prove yourselves brave and capable. Now is our time. Now is the time to unite. We will not be defeated."

"Get ready."

He waited until we all had our hands hovering over the map. Mine was over Karkatua again and he shifted it. This time to Far Port.

"Remember, wife," he snarled. "For the good of the Empire."

He slammed my finger onto the map.

CHAPTER NINE

The poem on the wall of the tower was echoing in my mind. I was certain there was a key to what was happening in that poem. The next verse was easy to remember.

Come in and fetch,

Hearts and Tales,

Hopes so bright.

The hum of my bees grew as the horrible swallowing feeling seemed to drag on and on and then with a pop that resounded in my ears, I was in the world. I blinked, wiping my face with my hands as I tried to get my bearings.

This time, I hoped to get more of a chance than just to write on paper. I had so many things to say. So much I wanted to do before I lost my opportunity and whatever this strange, testing magic was, it was giving me a hint of that opportunity.

I was standing beside two men as they looked out from the second-story window. I saw my older brother Oska first. I hadn't expected that I'd cry if I saw my brother again, and yet tears sprang to my eyes unbidden.

He was alive. He looked well, though his eyes were dark as if he hadn't been getting enough rest. He was holding a sleeping toddler and speaking earnestly to someone as they looked out from a second-story over a field of grass and laughing children.

There were more here than my nieces and nephews though I saw them, too. Asha and Falren, Doen and Casch, Glorie and Henessa – and more strange faces mixed in the playing and shrieking. I stumbled forward, wanting to drink it all in. It was like watching the dawn after a long night of illness – a night you thought would never end.

They were well. Somehow, Osprey had made good on his promise and brought them to safety and family. My heart ached to be near them again.

And when I realized who Oska was speaking with, the sun rose in that inner dawn and blazed into my heart.

"What is that?" Oska teased, raising an eyebrow at what Osprey was eating. Osprey's blue eyes lit for a moment before the joy faded again.

"Bread and honey. A little cinnamon. A little nutmeg. I've always been fond of honey but now …" he shook his head as if he couldn't form more words and I realized there were tears in his eyes. One of them spilled over, running down his dark skin. He sniffed hard to pull back the rest. Oska reached out and put a hand on his arm.

"I'm glad they are here safe," Osprey said, almost choking on the words.

"And can you not forgive your father?" Oska asked quietly. "He did bring them here, and you were worried about them. Even as you brought our children to this safe place so far from the conflict, you spoke of these others you'd left behind. To see them must restore your soul, as bringing my family to me restored mine."

Osprey laughed but there was no humor in his laugh. And when he bit into his honey bread there was only sorrow in his eyes. And that was wrong. My hunter was grave and serious, but not broken-hearted.

"She's out there somewhere. And if my father hadn't been so faithful to the Emperor, I would never have been pitted against my brother. And if I were not, he wouldn't have been obsessed with ruining everything I loved. These children wouldn't have suffered for all these years. And your sister wouldn't have been swept up in this madness."

Oska opened his mouth but Osprey waved his words away.

"She's out there somewhere," Osprey said. "Sometimes I can feel her and it's like she's in the same room as me."

"I am in the same room," I muttered, and though they couldn't hear me, Osprey turned to look at me with a quizzical look in his eyes.

"You looked for her. You scoured the area where they went in. What more could you possibly do?" Oska asked.

My heart soared … and fell. He'd looked for me. He'd searched. But he'd found nothing. And no wonder. The fires would have erased all trace. There would be no way to track us and the first outpost we found with the undertrails would have been utterly consumed by flames as well.

"At any rate," Osprey said, sucking in a long breath to steady himself. "It is best to keep my father well away. He claims not to be loyal to Juste Montpetit, but old habits die hard."

"Victore is finding him a useful source of information. He says he can continue to learn from him about the enemy's strategy."

"Victore," Osprey repeated the name and it sounded dismissive.

"Don't brush his judgment away. Yes, he's muddled, but it was his strategies that won that first day. And he is drawing up battle plans for the next strike. Whatever he may have forgotten, he has not lost his skill in tactics."

Osprey shrugged. "Even so, my father should not be so relied on. He has served the Winged Empire all his life."

"So, have you, brother," Oska said, tucking one of his little son's curls behind a sleepy ear. "And look at your pure heart. You'd never harm one of these. You're the only reason we still have them whole and safe."

My heart warmed when my brother called Osprey "brother" but at the same time, it mourned. Because I could see the faces that weren't there playing with the children. Helissa. Anfrea. I didn't let my mind list the rest. It would hurt too much. Be too hard.

Instead, I cried into my heart, into the feather that was tangled up in the Forbidding inside me. I sobbed into my bees, channeling all my sorrow and all my heart into them.

To my surprise, they swelled, bubbling up out of my hands and pouring out the window. They hurried in every direction and I had the strangest feeling that they were headed out to pollinate the world. My brow creased further and then one last bee slipped from my grasp and went to join my first one with Osprey.

They buzzed around his head, but he didn't swat them away. Instead, he reached out a finger so they could stand on it and whispered, "What news, little friends?"

"I'll leave you to talk to bees," Oska said with a good-natured laugh, patting Osprey on the shoulder.

I watched him go a little wistfully. If only I could speak to them. If only they could see me for one last goodbye.

But this was good. This was more than I could have asked for. I was blinking back tears now, too. This might be my last glimpse of Osprey. I hardly let myself blink. I didn't want to miss a second of it.

I felt my bees swelling out from me and my heart was with them as they spread toward the horizon. I joined Osprey at the window, distracted for a moment by what I saw. Just past that grassy field where the children were playing was the city of Far Port. I'd never seen it, but I recognized it from its description. But all around it, the Forbidding had crept in so close that there was barely room for city anymore. To that mass of darkness, my bees ventured. As if they hoped to fight back the madness all on their own.

And something in me seemed to light at that idea. Could they be right? What did bees do in the world? They went from flower to flower and because of them, something grew that wasn't there before. Could they spread the pollen of hope? Could it somehow combat darkness? It seemed crazy. But everything about this was crazy. Was it really insane to hope for something good?

If I was the queen of my hive, that was what I'd send out my worker bees to do. I'd send them out like an army to drive back darkness and judgment with mercy and hope.

I let that thought soar out from me.

"Be full of hope. Spread all that you can. Work together," I said, trying to strengthen them with my words. "Draw on this delight of living children of their joy and laughter and carry it with you. Heal our land. Please, heal our land!"

I paused and beside me, Osprey was still looking at my bees with an expression of rueful joy.

"She must still be out there somewhere if you are here," he whispered. "I wish you could speak to me. But maybe she can see me through you. Please tell her that I kept her nephews and nieces safe. Please tell her that the children I love are safe, too. I'm leaving them with Oska now. They will be cared for and loved. Raquella is coming to help."

My heart kicked up as he spoke with such love and care.

"I have to go back to the battle," he whispered to the bee. "What we started isn't done, and if I can't find her, I can at least fight for her land."

I moved in a little closer. He might not see me, but it felt – right – to stand this close. To see every little detail in the flickering changes of his expressions.

"There's so much more to be done. The army at Glorious Ingvar has surged forward. They plan to retake our cities. Wing Ivo and Victore are gathering our troops. There will be pitched battles and I must be there. Please, please tell her I love her. I wish I could have been free with her, but the freedom she bought for me has saved so many lives."

He looked away from the bees, turning wistful as he looked out at the children in the field and my heart melted.

When he turned back to the room, his blue eyes liquid with unshed tears, his bottom lip quivering lightly, I grew bold. I stepped forward and laid my spirit lips on his and kissed him.

He gasped and his eyes shut for a moment as he kissed me back and then they sprang open again as if he realized this was real.

"Honey," he gasped. "You always taste like honey and stings."

The tears that had been in his eyes slid down his cheeks and hit the roughness of his unshaven face. His lips bent into a crooked almost-smile and he swallowed, his hands coming up to hold me so lightly – as if I were a soap bubble about to pop.

I opened my lips to tell him that I loved him. To tell him I was grateful. I was proud.

The sensation of swallowing rolled over me like the grave.

"No, no, no."

Osprey was ripped from my grasp as the Forbidding pulled me back, tearing me from the world like a sapling from the ground. The last thing I saw was Osprey's smile and then I was back in the frozen tangle of the Forbidding, my heart shattering with despair.

CHAPTER TEN

I returned to the arm of the Forbidding with a gasp.

He'd felt me there. It was only for a moment, but he'd tasted my kiss. That was progress.

It felt like a punch to my belly. I had something to lose. I'd been so certain that I was walking to my own death that I'd been burying my heart and making myself ready. And suddenly, I wasn't ready again. I wanted to hold on. I wanted more kisses.

I forced my eyes open, trying to focus on something – anything – else to distract me from the sudden winds of longing blowing through my heart.

I was the first to awaken and to my surprise, the room we were in looked different. It was … green? It seemed green in the glow of our lights instead of just black. Green and brown as if it were the inside of a plant instead of just blackness. And tiny slivers of cracks were spidering along the edges of the tangles. They weren't wide enough to light the room, but they glowed a very faint green as if light wished it could get through the cracks.

The Seat of the Adder was green, too. And it glowed slightly around Juste's frozen form.

I bit my lip and tried to change positions, but my feet wouldn't move. Panic struck me. Something was holding my feet! Its grip was like a vice.

I twisted to look at them as I struggled against the pull. Could I draw the short sword? I reached for it at the same moment that I caught a glimpse of my feet. They were stuck in place by strands of the Forbidding. My breath caught in my chest and I shuddered. Held in place. Stuck.

With a gasp, I pulled my short sword from my sheathe and tried to saw at the strands, but there was no effect at all. It didn't even nick them. I felt – and oh but I hoped it was my imagination! – the Forbidding strand slip just a little higher up my leg.

My breath was coming quickly. My heart pounding so very fast. I was trapped. There would be no way out except these tests. The Hissan hadn't expected us to get free. I should never have hoped for it either. But I did hope and it was like someone had taken an apple corer to my heart. There was nothing left of it but an empty space.

I clawed for my wrist and reached in to feel Os's icy cold feather. Even the cold was a relief because it was his feather. It was the symbol of Osprey's affection for me – that he wanted me to stay safe, that he'd put some small part of himself with me to remind me of that.

My head was swimming and I was still clutching the feather inside the cuff when I heard the squeak of someone else realizing they were stuck. I wiggled my way back up and into my chair. At least I could get trapped by the Forbidding in a seat, right?

It was Essena. Her face, when she looked up at me, was grey in the light of her owl manifestation.

"You, too?" she asked tightly.

I nodded. "The sword doesn't cut it."

I should feel compassion for her – but I didn't. She could have fought for the Winged Empire without spying on us. Without betraying my brother. Without orchestrating his death. She hadn't. If she died here with me, she deserved it for what she'd done.

"Don't look at me like that," she said disdainfully. "If it weren't for me you wouldn't have that crown."

I opened my mouth to snap back as her owl dove for the strands, screeching. There was a tearing sound and then it soared upward, shaking slightly, and dove again. Again and again and again in frenzied attacks, growing smaller and smaller with each one. I was stunned as I watched Essena crumple, her shoulders shaking with silent sobs. She'd hoped to live, too.

I swallowed. Maybe I did feel compassion after all.

And then Juste unfroze. He evaluated his feet. He looked at the short sword still in my hand and the strands of Forbidding still very much around my ankles.

"Can't cut it?" he asked with a lifted brow.

"We're here until the end," I confirmed.

He looked at Essena. "No help from your bird?"

Her owl was nothing more than a flicker on her shoulder. She shook her head, not even looking up.

His nod was definitive. "Then we play this out."

Xectare and the Eagle woke at the same moment and came to the same realization as we had. Xectare, with her usual coolness. The Eagle with a look of panic in his eye.

"Don't fight it," Juste ordered them. "You'll just wear yourself out."

His mouth twisted as he shot a look of condemnation at Essena. He hated weakness. Which was surprising, since he surrounded himself with so many people who appeared strong but were weak where it counted.

We waited on the Raven. And waited. And waited.

Juste's hiss snapped all our gazes to him. He was staring at the Raven, frozen over the table, her finger still set on the map.

"So," he said. "A test is not a test unless some fail. Report."

She wasn't going to come back to life, I realized with a gasp. That was the price of failure. Being frozen in time like that. Not taken by the Forbidding but taken somehow by its magic.

And just like that, her death was dismissed.

"Our battle goes poorly. More and more houses defect to the traitors," the Eagle said heavily. He seemed to be weighing his words and there was something in his eyes when he looked at Juste. "They say you are dead. That your rule is –"

His voice cut off abruptly as the snake shot out from Juste, hissing in front of him. His eagle shrieked, diving down as if on its own, and at the last second he threw his hand up and stopped it. The snake stayed back, threatening, but not acting yet.

"I was able to speak," the Eagle choked out. "Toward the end. I spoke and I assured their leaders that you live. That they owe you their fealty."

The snake retreated.

"And you, wife?" Juste spun to me. "Did you convince anyone of my sovereignty?"

I shook my head. I could lie but not about that. It would be too easy for him to find me out. "I heard a rumor that General Petren has come to Far Stones."

I needed to give him something.

"Who did you hear it from?" he asked, his voice low and vicious.

I couldn't tell him I'd heard it from Osprey. I needed to hide that his brother lived. Though I couldn't quite figure out why I needed to hide that.

At the thought of his name, my bee flickered and I saw a quick glimpse of him on a broad field. He was pointing around himself at land features while a group of men with a single wing stitched on their coats listened to him. I blinked and the vision was gone.

"One of my brothers," I said in a rush. "They hear things. It was only a rumor."

"And did you tell this brother anything?"

I shook my head.

"You try my patience, wife." His face was stiff, and he tapped his fingers on the side of the table as if deciding what to do with me.

"What is she here for if not to feed you, Le Majest?" Wing Xectare said. And there was a glitter in her eye. She was hiding something, too. Using me to distract from it. What a nest of snakes we all were. "Why not take her power for the next test."

He paused, seeming to consider it as he licked his upper lip. And then he pounced on me, reaching across and plunging his hand into my neckline. His palm hit the feather and like every time before he pulled. I swayed as the power left me, leaving me clutching the edge of the table for support. I could barely sit straight.

Exhausted, I lay my forehead on the table as Wing Xectare explained that this time she was able to speak to one of her apprentices and tell her to prepare to deliver orders from Le Majest to the leaders of the Claws in Glorious Ingvar. That they were to use the weapons she had hidden there for the defense of the city and tell all who would listen that Juste Montpetit lived and would reward his faithful. She was such a good Wing.

Essena had made contact with the Single Wing, still claiming to work for them. She said they were close to losing Astar Harbor and were nervous about Karkatua falling with it. Talking about it seemed to restore her strength and her eyes glittered as she spoke.

"So, now we have the information we need to channel into a strategy," Juste said. "And surely this is what we are being tested in. The Adder must be able to rule the world. It is fitting that the magic tests my ability to do so. This will be our strategy. We will push our troops to take Astar Harbor and then Karkatua. When they are captured, our armies must march further west and take back the rest of what has been lost. You must tempt your Single Wing into failure, Wing Essena. We do not want this drawn out or who knows how long we'll be stuck in the test. Eagle, those on the mainland must be strengthened so they lose fewer houses. Remind them there are no other options, Eagle. Remind them that I am the only blood of the Emperor. If I die, what will they do? Be reigned by this settler?" he pointed to me to emphasize his point. "And you, Empress." He looked at me with a sneer. "You are so diminished I expect little. Simply do not get in my way." He turned his gaze to each of us. "We go again. Work harder this time. Don't be like the Raven."

"Of course not, Le Majest," Wing Xectare said respectfully.

He took my hand in his. "This time, you are coming with me."

He placed both of our fingers on Astar Harbor and the sense of swallowing made me choke down bile.

CHAPTER ELEVEN

Open with blood,

Pay our price,

Bind your eyes.

The words of the next verse from the tower rippled through my mind. Last time they had been accurate. After all, I had fetched hope in seeing my Osprey again. But this prophecy felt less welcoming. Open with blood? Pay the price? I was already swaying from the energy Juste had stolen from me.

The world shuddered into being and I felt like I was being vomited out of the Forbidding. I stood right on the edge of it – but also on the edge of a pitched battle rolling out over a plain. In the distance, I saw Astar Harbor, flags snapping crisply in the wind, boats and ships gathered far from the city as if fleeing the conflict.

They'd talked about a fight for Astar Harbor. This was that fight. Out there somewhere, Juste would be trying to marshal his troops to press for victory. And the other Wings would help him. Thankfully, he had not ended up in the same place as me, even though he had grabbed my hand to force me to be there with him.

But that might be the only thing to be thankful for. I walked like a ghost between fallen men and women, dead in a blood-soaked carpet across the muddy fields. My breath hitched in my throat. It was always going to come to this – war. A pitched battle between us and them. Us for our freedom. Them to keep us from it. Why did they want that enough to fight us? Was it really worth their lives?

I stumbled, trying not to look at faces. And then I stopped myself from that nonsense. Of course, I should look at faces. What if no one else did? What if I was the only one who saw them in death and truly cared?

There was a boy who looked about my age. He clutched his wounded belly, but his eyes stared far away, curtained by death.

There was an older woman. She could be my older sister Anfrea. Her hair was splayed around her sightless face. Was she someone else's sister? Someone's mother?

My eyes were getting glassy. I blinked back tears and shuddered. All of this death. All unnecessary. It didn't have to be this way. But they'd forced us to it. They'd taken everything except our lives and thought we'd be grateful just to keep those. No, they hadn't even let us keep our lives because were they really even our lives if we couldn't defend them? If we couldn't live them with free minds and free tongues? No. They were just pale shadows. Death on the front step instead of fully in the door.

I shook my head, tears pouring from my eyes. It was right to feel their deaths. If I didn't who would? Who was going to remember these sacrifices? Who was going to mourn?

My bees began to buzz in my heart as my fury built.

There was a shout ahead and I looked up.

I'd stumbled further than I thought. Before my eyes, the Claws – their blue uniforms trimmed in stark white – pressed the revolutionaries back. Someone was beating a drum and they seemed to be moving in time with it. Most of the revolutionaries had sewn a wing into the fabric of what they wore – but it was easy enough to see who didn't wear blue. The Claws were pushing hard to gain a hill that the Single Wing had taken. As I watched, they swept over like a wave, the dark sky behind them billowing with blackened clouds as if to signify how the skies felt about this battle. Tiny spears of light shot golden and pure between those rumbling towers, but they were few and the battlefield was as dark as it was bloody and churning.

The scent of blood and offal was heavy in the air and I choked on it as I stumbled forward, one of my hands clasped over my nose and mouth. The sounds all around me, shouting and screaming, battle cries and dull moans – they made me feel as if I was on a boat rocked back and forth on the waves. I couldn't quite get my bearings.

Behind the battle in front of me – just barely visible, I saw the clash of a bright orange eagle and some other spirit bird in the sky. The other bird was faintly purple. Was it … could it be Osprey?

My heart skipped a beat and I nearly choked when my breathing stuttered and then started again. Sparks flew from the pair as they crashed together and then disappeared in the roiling clouds.

I felt my bees surge within me, and I was surprised. I'd expected to be destitute of magic after Juste had sucked out my strength, and yet they poured from me in a cloud of golden specks, buzzing and humming with the joy of life in stark relief against the battlefield around us.

My mouth fell open at the sight of them. My breath seizing in my chest. I could help. I could do this.

I picked up my feet and began to run, charging down the battlefield toward where our people clashed against the Claws. I slipped and skidded through the churning mud and trampled grass, avoiding the fallen as much as I could. Someone moved, moaning and I almost stopped, but I couldn't stay here long. And if I stopped to help I'd be swallowed by the Forbidding before I could do anything of value. I had to work quickly on what could be done.

Behind the clash of forces, in the distance, but close enough that it could be a problem if I wasn't careful, a fat green spirit-snake slid across the battlefield. It snatched up a fleeing Single Wing fighter and swallowed him in a single gulp. Juste was up there.

I ran faster.

A mounted Single Wing fighter led the countercharge on the hill, fist raised over his head. With a roar, he crashed into the wave of Claws, his companions spread out behind him like a cape. Their shouts joined his and my heart sped to catch them.

I tried to keep track of the details as they crashed into the enemy, but between my pounding feet jarring my vision and the need to watch where I was stepping to keep from tripping over fallen friends and foes, I missed most of it.

By the time I looked up, the fighter had been dragged from his horse. It reared up, screaming and pawing the air as the Claws beat back the remaining Single Wing.

No. They couldn't take this hill. From where I ran, I could see it all playing out. The moment this hill was gone, the Claws wouldn't have to defend this flank and they'd wrap around and take our armies from behind to the south of here. My head swiveled back and forth as I ran studying the field. There was no other force of rebels close to here who could take this back or push through once this hill was claimed. Either the Single Wing won here, or the tide of this battle would turn and the whole army would be routed.

I pushed harder, my legs screaming from the effort. This mustn't be allowed to happen. It mustn't. All thoughts of spirit birds and snakes in the distance faded away and it was just this fight here – these people here – that filled my mind.

The horse was fleeing, running right toward me. But I'd been dealing with horses all my life. It had to slow to cross over a gully right in front of me and as it slowed, slipping on what was in the gully – I didn't want to know what – I took that moment to seize its bridle and leap. Maybe the bees helped. Or maybe it was luck. But I landed square in the saddle, snatching up the flapping reins and pulling the mare in. She snorted, tossing her head in irritation and fear, but I turned her with neat nudges and careful reining.

She was strong and uninjured, more fearful than hurt. Her powerful muscles bunched under me as she spun, fighting the reins.

"Easy, girl. Easy. We aren't done yet. We've got to go back. Easy."

I had her stepping forward again in a blink, and then brought her up to a canter again, back toward where the Claws were beating back the Single Wing.

"Come on now, don't fail me now," I said, drawing my short sword and holding it high as I bellowed wordless defiance against our enemy.

The searing heat in the cuff of my sleeve gave me strength to push forward. Out there somewhere, Osprey was fighting. He was probably close for the feather to burn like that. This battle was for him.

Around me, the bees swirled, and we charged forward, forward, sweeping across the ground and through our dodging allies toward the enemy. My bees took the brunt of the crash, but I slipped in behind them, slashing and hacking. And I tried to forget it was people I was slicing with my sword – someone's father, someone's son. And tried to think only of fighting the Forbidding – the grasping tangles of dark magic that would rip me apart if they could.

This army would do the same. They'd tried to rend my people with their laws and strictures. They were trying again in war. It was only my bees and my sword that could fight them.

Behind me, I heard something that was both warcry and cheer. If hope had a sound, this would be it, roaring from throats, crashing across the ears of our enemies as our blades crashed with theirs. The Single Wing fighters had joined me in the fight, pressing forward side by side with me.

Something sharp bit my leg. Pain seared through me, but still, I fought, eyes blinded to all but the moment, the fight right in front of me, the duck and lunge, parry and slash. Men and women in blue coats fell screaming and when no one else fell I drew my horse up and tried to catch my breath.

Heat soaked my leg and pain filled me like jagged glass. My blood spilled down my leg, dripping to the earth below in thick red spatters. My bees had protected me from the worst of the clash, but they couldn't turn a sword blade – and now they were rushing away, dispersing across the field, not before me but out to the side toward the Forbidding, just like they had last time. I could almost feel a hum of energy from them that echoed with the hum of those still out there at Far Port spreading the pollen of hope. I shook my head, trying to clear it.

Another group of fighters charged toward us and I braced myself, realizing only at the last minute that they were Single Wing and not more Claws.

"We have the hill!" one of them yelled and around me, there were greetings and excited exclamations and people seeing to the wounded, but I had eyes for only one thing – the purplish-white bird sailing up from behind them.

Os was bigger than I remembered, and he carried his manifestor with powerful flaps of his spirit-wings. Osprey's gaze caught on mine and his lips parted in a gasp. He never even slowed. He snatched me from the horse, lifting me up on the wings of his bird and wrapping me tightly in his arms.

"You're here in the flesh this time," he marveled.

I didn't bother to look at where we were going or who might be watching. I only had eyes for my desperate Osprey. He had a new scar down one cheek and his blue eyes carried a depth of new sadness. A toothpick hung from his lower lip as if it had claimed the spot for itself. I plucked it away.

"My hunter," I breathed.

"And your bees are with you," his eyes lit, and he leaned in, as if he was drawing my scent in and memorizing it. He leaned his forehead to mine, closing his eyes to satisfied slits. "Are you back, House Apidae? Are you really here?"

"Not for long," I admitted. "The end is close."

He opened his mouth, and I was sure he had more questions, but I would be gone in a moment and I didn't want to be gone. I wanted to be here – with him. I wanted to stay here forever, even in the middle of a battle, even with everything hanging in the balance. My bees spun around us in a golden cloud, buzzing as if this was all they wanted, too.

I clung to him like a child, kissing his cheek, his forehead, his mouth, in small soft kisses as if I could eat him up and never have to let go of him.

After a moment I broke from him and he looked long into my eyes. "Do you visit me from the grave House Apidae, or do you yet live? Do not misunderstand. If you visit me only for a moment from beyond the lands of the living, still I am satisfied to hold you one last time."

I swallowed. "I'm alive – with your brother and three others. We are being tested by the Forbidding, but none of us are expected to escape its grasp. I don't know if I'll see you again, so I think I should thank you now."

He was shaking his head. "No thanks are ever needed between us."

"Thank you for my family. For guarding them." I knew my tears were flowing and he was still trying to comfort me, taking my face in his hands and wiping my tears with his thumbs. "Thank you for their lives."

Around us, there was nothing but stormy sky, and swirling yellow bees, and the white wings of Os, and I wanted it to stay like this forever.

"If you live, House Apidae, I will find you. I will come to you and cut down your foes." His eyes had gone dark now and the sadness was replaced by something else. Grim determination, I thought. He let go of my face and wrapped me up in his strong arms, his embrace protective and almost too tight, as if he was trying to hold me there, too.

But what if he really did come looking? We were hidden here. Even if you knew where this place was, could you enter it? It had taken the last of Essa's life to make a door for us. I saw him in my mind's eye hunting for me for years. Growing old. Wasting away. His life spent on a useless hope. I choked on a sob.

"It's too late, my hunter. You'll never find me in time." I needed to be selfless. If I loved freedom so much, I needed to give him his. "Stay here. Find happiness again. Raise little ones and enjoy them."

I removed my finger, sad the moment it left his soft lips. I was going to miss the feel of those. I shouldn't be touching him more after trying to say goodbye, but I couldn't help myself, I leaned in and kissed him again, trying to fill the kiss with all my admiration for him, all my delight, all the desperate longings of a soul that wished it could be with him forever. And I tried to put into it the goodbye I couldn't say. He pressed something into my hand, and I took it. Holding it tight but refusing to break our kiss. Why should it end? Why should something so perfect ever end?

And then I felt the swallowing of the Forbidding and something within me broke as it dragged me from his arms, pulling me back, forcing me to return.

I was shaking with sobs as it tore me apart and threw me back to my place at the table. A place where the tangles of Forbidding now grasped me all the way to the waist. My leg was still bleeding, pouring a trickle of blood onto the ground. If only I was the Adder this could be the end. Blood on the rocks. A price paid.

Pain flared in my hand and I opened my palm. To my shock, a toothpick was clutched in my palm. I stared at it as my sobs intensified and my last hope scattered like the fluff of a dandelion in a stiff breeze.

CHAPTER TWELVE

In this place, I had only one bee. All the rest were torn from me and I felt my energy leave me again the moment I returned to my body at the table. Juste had drained me here, and here I was still drained.

I could still feel Osprey's kiss on my lips. I closed my eyes for just a moment and savored it. My lip trembled a little as I held back emotion.

Okay, Aella. Now you get up and fight again.

But I could barely move my head from the rim of the table. It lolled lifelessly. And yet, there was a warmth in me that I couldn't describe. I'd seen him again. He lived. I'd been able to say goodbye. Who could wish for more than that?

After a moment, I opened my eyes. I felt for the wound in my leg. It seemed big but I couldn't tell how deep it was. My hand came away wet with blood.

My one lone bee hopped down from the table to buzz around my leg. Perhaps it could patch the wound.

"Please try," I whispered. "Please try."

Something brushed the back of my neck and I shuddered and then choked as a noose wrapped around my neck. No, not a noose – a snake. It yanked my head up so that Juste's eyes could bore into me, furious and dark.

"Did you think I would not see? You interfered with us. You fought against us." He gritted his teeth. He was wounded, too. I saw blood bubbling up from a slash to his shoulder. It would need stitches – but there was nothing to stitch it with. His arm was shaking from the shock, but still, his focus was on me. I didn't even get a chance to look around the table before he snatched my hand again. My head was spinning from exhaustion and pain. "We will go back, Wings, and we will turn that tide for the Empire of War and Wings, and you Empress, will go somewhere safe where you can do no harm."

"Perhaps it would be better if she didn't go a all," Xectare's voice suggested. So. She lived still. I tried to twist to see her, but Juste's snake kept me in place, eyes fixed on him alone.

"We all go until we die," Juste said through gritted teeth. "I will defeat this enemy. And you will do your part to help me."

He took my hand and jammed it toward the map – to the continent, to a random spot on the map outside Kestrel City. "You'll cause no trouble there."

But at the last second, I yanked my hand with all the power I had left and let it land on Far Stones instead. I didn't even catch a glimpse of where it was as my vision blurred and his angry curses filled the air. The swallowing began again.

It was more painful than ever. As if the Forbidding was trying to digest me this time instead of just swallow me. Everything hurt from my wounded leg to my aching heart and up into the thunder pounding through my head. Perhaps all of this was finally taking its toll on me. My mouth was dry, in desperate need of a drink, and my belly ached the long ache of hunger.

The next lines of the poem from the door spiraled through my mind. I didn't dare ignore them. They'd been right every time so far. After all, hadn't I just left my blood all over the battlefield back in Astar Harbor?

Lose what you love,

Empty and cold,

It all grows old.

I flinched from the words. I didn't want to lose what I loved. I was doing all this to prevent that. I was doing all this to keep my family safe. It was why I fought. I refused to lose them. And I refused to lose the freedom I'd helped to bring for them.

I fell to the hard stone floor, rolling as I was vomited from the mouth of the Forbidding and I realized – with horror – that I had exited a literal tangle of Forbidding that was reaching in and through and all around a city wall.

I struggled to my feet. I was balanced along the wall. There were long, wailing screams from within the city and just as many from without. It was night, but there were fires burning everywhere – enough that I could see clearly in the dark and light flicker of the flames. Was this Astar Harbor? Was the fight still going on?

But no. It was certainly not that. I knew this city. I could see the spirit-tower rising from the Western edge of it – invisible to most eyes. I could see the Oriole fountain and the district burned to ash around it. I was on the walls of Glorious Ingvar. And the battle was raging all around me. Both sides looked scattered. Leader-less. One group of blue-coated fighters fought a ragged band of Single Wing, but though there was another band of Single Wing rushing past on the other side, they didn't stop to help. Perhaps they didn't see their brothers. Perhaps they did and chose to make another target their aim.

And that's what I saw everywhere. Chaos. A lack of cohesion. And people wounded, dying. In agony. Alone.

I bit my lip as the rage bubbled up and through me. This wasn't supposed to be this way. It shouldn't have come to this.

"They called for unity after Astar Harbor," a thready voice said from the ground beside me. I looked down and almost stumbled in my haste to drop to my knees.

Wing Ivo lay there, a sword plunged through his side. He clung to it with one hand and to a banner with a flag on the end of it in the other. I realized, after a moment, that the shadows around us were littered with bodies. No one else but Ivo stirred.

"Unity with what?" I asked gently, feeling his brow. He was cold but sweating.

"Unity for all people on Far Stones," he gasped, and I didn't know if he even realized he was speaking to me or if he was just speaking out into the air. "They called on all people to drop their weapons, turn them in, stop revolting, and submit to be registered. They say they want peace. They want unity. If we do it their way."

I nearly rolled my eyes. That must have been Juste's idea. It sounded like him. He was exactly the kind of person who would want unity and peace – as long as it was his unity, his peace. The kind where he dominated and everyone else submitted.

"And you said?" I asked gently.

"We said we'd pay for our freedom with our blood if necessary." There was blood now, on his lips. A little bubble of it in the corner of his mouth.

I sank lower so that his drooping eyelids could see me. "What can I do?"

"Aella," he gasped, groaning. His eyes shut for a moment in a wince and then he was looking at me. "A Wing tells an apprentice when she is a Wing. Usually, there is a ceremony."

"Is there a ceremony for the apprentice to tell the Wing that she's grateful?" I asked gently. No amount of rage could fix this, though I felt it bubbling within me, stinging my eyes with unshed tears. "To tell him that he changed everything for her? That he was a father when her father was gone?"

He smiled, his glassy eyes looking to me. "It really is you. When Osprey said he saw you, I was sure it was a vision. Sure it was a fool's errand for him to go chasing after you."

"Chasing after me?" I felt both cold and hot at the thought. But maybe it was just the ravings of a dying man. I needed to focus on him not on me and my hopes. I took his hand in mine.

"The flag," he moaned. "The flag needs to go up."

He pointed to a place over the city gate where a flag holder was set. It was empty now.

"To rally the troops. To end chaos. We need it. Victore told me to do whatever it took."

And he had done that. My eyes were thick with tears. One of them splashed on his jacket.

At his shoulder, a ghost of Harpy flickered into existence and then was gone again. Just a glimmer of gold in the darkness. Ivo couldn't sustain a manifestation.

"I'm going to try to heal you with my bees," I said, and my tongue felt like it was stumbling all over itself. It was too thick. Words were too unwieldy right now. I reached out to the hum of my bees and they came to me in a golden cloud.

"No," he gasped. "It's too late for me. But the flag must fly."

Again, there was a little flash of Harpy as if Ivo was trying to call his friend for help.

"I can do both," I said, my lip trembling.

"The flag," he insisted, trying to lift the flagpole.

I hurried to take it from his hand.

"I see your bees everywhere," he whispered softly, as I took the flag gently from his hands. "They are tiny lights in the darkness, all through the Forbidding. I see them everywhere. They are working on something. Something massive. I think that's what drove him to it. Every time he saw one all he could think of was the manifestor."

"Who saw them?" I asked gently.

"The flag!" he said urgently, almost raving now. "Put it up while I can still see. Let me know I succeeded."

I nodded. "Of course. I'll be right back."

I rushed to where the flag holder was, leaping over bodies and trying not to slip. I had to lean well over the edge of the wall to put the flag in place. My injured leg screamed at me. It had opened again and was spilling blood everywhere. I had to hurry and get this done for Wing Ivo, for my friend.

I almost fell as I leaned over the wall but my cloud of bees pushed me back onto my feet as I jammed the flag in place.

As if they were only waiting for that, the bees scattered, flying in every direction. Some of them directly into the tangle of Forbidding that had eaten through the city wall, others floating out across the horizon.

Below us, I heard the roar of voices and a battle cry. "For the Single Wing!"

Could a flag really make that much of a difference?

"Freedom!" they cried.

I didn't stay to watch them. I hurried back to Ivo. I must have enough of my bees left to try to heal him. They'd done more than that before. They could help. Just like with Juste. Just like with Osprey. I skidded to my knees beside him.

"Wing Ivo?" I asked gently.

But when I met his eyes they were glazed over with death.

My hands shook so hard that I had to clutch them to my chest, No. Not more death. Not more loss.

I couldn't take even one more.

Tears streaked hot down my cheeks and I collapsed on the ground beside him.

I was tired. I was so tired. And all of this for what? One atrocity only led to the next and the next. One battle to another and another.

I just wanted to put my head down and sleep it all away.

The jaws of the Forbidding closed around me and the swallowing began again, and no amount of tears could stop it.

CHAPTER THIRTEEN

I felt oddly empty when I returned to the table. So much so, that I didn't even bother to sigh when I realized that the twists of the Forbidding had crawled up to my chest, wreathing me in its writhing embrace.

I sniffed hard as I tried to wipe the tears from my eyes before the rest of them woke.

I took a moment to try to get my mind back in order. Everyone else was still frozen. I was the first one back. Perhaps they'd laid out a plan after I'd rebelled. Perhaps they were enacting it. I sighed, feeling the pain in my bleeding leg and the exhaustion making my whole body heavy. I felt like I'd been awake for months. Like if I fell asleep, I'd never wake again. And yet, it had only been a few hours in here. It couldn't have been more than that, could it?

I blinked wearily and took comfort in one thing – the rebels had pushed the battle to Glorious Ingvar. That meant they were winning. They were gaining ground. There was hope for those I had left behind outside this place. But the Forbidding was creeping right into their cities. If we didn't deal it a final blow here, that would be the end of the rebellion – the end of everyone in the Far Stones settlement and the end of all I loved.

I needed to hold my courage and be firm. In my mind, my bees still buzzed and it seemed like there were so very many of them, and yet they were so, so far away, each with a tiny piece of me kept in them. I'd left a cloud of them out there every time I'd been brought out in the testing. And they were still out there somewhere. What would happen if there was none of me left to give next time? Would I run out of bees or would I run out of Aella?

The cracks in the walls of the Forbidding around us were larger now. I could stick my arm between them if I wanted to. Through them, I saw the sun setting, shining golden beams. I tried to peer out of one to see if I could see anyone or anything, but all I could make out was sun and leaves and stone and tangled Forbidding.

With a gasp like one rising from the dead, Wing Xectare awoke, her bright eyes glittering from across the table. Her swan swam over her head but its usual placid glide stuttered.

"Still alive, aberration?" she asked, and her voice was cracked and weak.

"For now," I said, letting my eyes narrow to slits. "What were you doing in the wide world, Xectare?"

"That's Swan to you," she said, coughing as she tried to get her voice back. She tried to lean forward, but in the grasp of the Forbidding, she couldn't move. When she was finished, she continued. "The Emperor gave us our names after you rebelled. We are above you now."

"That's nice," I said acidly. I pointed at the Forbidding wrapped around her chest. "Would you say that you're winning, then?"

She snarled but she was saved from having to answer by Juste waking. He was speaking even before his dizziness passed. I could tell because his gaze sought mine but couldn't catch it.

"You thwart me at every turn, nemesis. Even married to me, you will not bend or bow. But your blood will mark this rock. Your death will release this world."

I swallowed. "You're mad."

He shook his head. "What do you think they do to the person who gets the memories? I figured it out on my way to this place. They need a blood sacrifice when this is all over and the test is passed. The memory will show you that eventually. You are that sacrifice, Empress. Why else did you think I would marry you?"

"To keep me close," I whispered.

"Yes. I needed you to be here so I could offer you at just the right time," he said with a nod. "Why else do you think I would be obsessed with you?"

"Because you hate your brother," I said with a tremble in my throat. "And he wanted me."

"My poor sad brother. He died at just the right time."

My eyes flickered to the Eagle, frozen beside the table. He knew that Osprey was not dead. Had he failed to report that? He hadn't moved yet. I looked to where his finger pointed to the map. It was still on Astar Harbor. He hadn't made it back from the trip where he fought Osprey on the battlefield. Had his failure to kill my beloved also been his failure to pass the Forbidding's test?

And now I had a secret I didn't dare tell. Because if Juste didn't know Osprey lived, then maybe, just maybe, Osprey would be able to surprise him one of these times, and that might be enough to tip this balance and help me win. A tiny flare of hope surged through me.

"There is one more time that we go into the map. And then

you die," Juste said. "And this time, I'm taking no chances."

His snake slipped out and grabbed my hand, binding it tightly in its coils. I reached with my other hand and froze. It was bound in the Forbidding, and tug as I might, it would not come free.

Juste began to laugh.

"You've lost your Wings one by one," I said, meeting his eyes with mine. "You've lost your cities one by one, too. But you can never win because you were never willing to sacrifice yourself, only other people. Where is Essena? Where is the Eagle? Gone because you'd rather give them than yourself."

He wasn't laughing anymore. A pleasant smile was on his face, but his eyes burned with fury. His voice was a growl.

"Let's put you somewhere safe this time. No more rallying banners that turn the tide of war. No more famous stands on hills."

The snake drew my hand over the map and though I fought it, it was too powerful. It set my finger close to Kestral City on the main continent and shoved my hand down.

And this time, I could hear the voice of the Forbidding, repeating the next lines of the poem to me.

LAY BARE YOUR DESIRE

GREAT OR SMALL

GAIN IT TWICE

"What's happening to the people who don't come out of the test?" I asked, as the darkness covered me. If it was going to talk to me, perhaps it could be useful.

THEY HAVE BEEN SIFTED.

"And?" I asked as the swallowing sensation began.

THERE IS NOTHING LEFT TO SIFT.

I shivered. Wing Essena hadn't woken up. Neither had the Eagle or the Raven. They had been sifted. There had been nothing left.

Little creeping sensations went up my spine at the thought and I hoped it was only my fear and not more of the Forbidding encasing me.

For some reason, I saw in my mind the face of my friend Zayana lit bright by her red bird Flame. In my mind, she was singing. And her song lifted my heart. She'd been sifted by her time in Far Stones and come out stronger and bolder. Beside her was my brother Retger, more thoughtful and protective than I remembered, sifted by all his family had suffered. And beside them, my Osprey, his eyes dark and haunted. All of life had been a long sifting for him – and yet there was still more and more of him left.

Just because we were being tested didn't mean we had to fail. Just because it was hard, didn't mean we couldn't triumph. Just because others had fallen didn't mean we had to break.

When the Forbidding spat me out, I was surprised to see people. I'd thought that Juste had picked a place where there would be no one at all.

To my shock, and the obvious shock of those around me, I was standing in the center of a field. I smelled something fecund and earthy that I didn't recognize. I thought it might be the trees nearby with their leaves as long as I was tall. I'd only ever seen paintings of trees like that.

On one side of me were five people in armor. Two of them

carried standards that had banners for five different houses on each one. The mouth of the one nearest me hung open. He was decked in feathers all the way from a ruff around his neck to the plumes hanging around the shoulders of his plate-metal breastplate. Beside him, a woman in a more feminine shape of plate mail stood holding a halberd in one hand, her other hand thrust out so that a spirit-falcon could sit on her wrist. The falcon was a dim teal color. It looked so much like an Osprey that my heart did a quick flip in my breast.

On my other side, Ixtap was arrayed with a pair of vultures and two sputtering men I could only believe were Winged Empire loyalists.

"What is the meaning of this?" one of the sputtering men said. "You bring another beyond who was agreed on? Shall our peace talks end here?"

"The crown," the woman with the falcon gasped, looking up at the crown of the Winged Empire on my head. She made the sign of the bird and sank to her knees.

Beside her, the others fell down in the same way. Their voices were reverent. "The crown."

"It's a trap," the same man said, but this time his voice wavered.

"It is no trap," I said calmly. "I am Aella of House Shrike, wife to Juste Montpetit, crowned Empress of the Winged Empire in Glorious Ingvar of the Far Stones. If I am not mistaken, you have been fighting for my husband's right to the throne."

His jaw snapped shut and without a word he and the vultures to either side reluctantly made their signs of the bird. There were no bows from them. I hadn't expected there to be.

But what surprised me the most was the look on Ixtap's face. He looked as if he were seeing his own ghost.

"You," he said, shock in his voice. "Are you the gift of Somm?"

And all of a sudden, a memory came to me. A memory that made sense of everything.

I saw a man clad only in snakeskin breeches. He was middle-aged and wiry, and he stood on the edge of the Forbidding, his eyes troubled.

"What will you do, Somm?" the woman beside him asked. "This is madness."

"Eventually, the Adder will come. And his blood will be shed to kill the Forbidding. But how will we know he is ready to sacrifice himself?" Somm asked. "How will we know that at the last minute he will give up his own life to free the people's souls, to offer his life for theirs? There must be a test. A way to sift and winnow out anyone who wouldn't make that final sacrifice. Otherwise, he might turn and instead enslave us all."

"What does that have to do with you?" It sounded like she was pleading. She looked out over a gathered group around her and many of them were reaching toward Somm as if they could stop what he was doing.

"I must build a test. A way to sift any who come. So that only the one willing to give their life will be let through. It must be done right."

"How could you possibly do that?" she asked, shaking her head.

"Trust me," he said with a smile. "And when the Adder comes, let all who wish to follow come in with him. For surely one will be worthy."

"The Adder will be worthy," she insisted. "You do not need to sacrifice yourself, Somm."

"Watch for my gift. It will come from an impossible distance at a moment of turning. It will be a miracle," he said, raising his voice to the gathered crowd. "Stand vigil for it. I will make our victory certain."

He didn't even say goodbye. He was sprinting off into the tangle of the Forbidding before anyone could stop him.

I blinked as I returned from the memory and looked Ixtap full in the eyes. "I think so, yes."

And he fell to his knees.

"Where did you come from?" one of the Vultures asked, eyebrows drawn downward. "You appeared from thin air."

I waved the question off. "There isn't time to explain the magic behind my arrival. What are you doing here?"

They were all looking at me and for the first time in all of this, I felt nervous – small. These were the important people of the Winged Empire. These were the people who made choices for my people – whose success helped us succeed, whose failures cost us everything. The very people we were rebelling against. They were all looking to me.

"You have been fighting on behalf of my husband the Emperor," I said to the group with Ixtap. Then I turned to the other group with the banners. "And you have been fighting against his rule because he has not yet appeared to you."

The man nearest me spoke. "We have brokered a truce, but we came here today hoping to agree on who should wear that crown. There has been no word of Juste Montpetit in almost a year. Surely, another must be found to take his place."

I held back the shudder. Almost a year? That couldn't be right. I thought Juste was sending birds to them with messages? Wasn't there one to tell him his father had died?

"The Emperor and I are fighting a battle against this dark magic – the Forbidding. We will not survive this battle." It was hard to say those words. Hard to admit what I didn't want to be true for me. There was a gasp from around me as my words sank in. "And here men are dying fighting over an Emperor who will never return to this place."

"That can't be true," one of the Vultures said, shaking his head.

"I can't solve your fights," I said, "but I can beg of you to seek peace."

They began to rise. The closest of them was the man with the feathered ruff who clearly led the rebel houses.

"You are not dead yet," he said roughly.

A memory filled my mind. A memory of Zayana whispering to Retger, I still believe more is possible.

I removed the Winged Crown from my head and handed it to him. "I am not, so hear my wishes. Give this crown to Zayana of House Cardinal, who loves this land and will lead it with dignity. She was trained to this but she is from outside this conflict. Anyone appointed from among you will bring with them the trail of the deeds done in this civil war. You need someone who has had no part in it."

I didn't know where the words came from – maybe because I really trusted Zayana, or maybe because she was the only one who was a part of their world who I trusted. At least she would have Retger with her, if nothing else. And my brother was honor through to the bones.

"Empress," one of the Vultures said from beside me. "The crown makes you our rightful ruler, but it is not for you to say who takes your place upon your death."

I spun to face him, gripping my hands together to keep from chickening out. I was crazy to be speaking to rulers like this. Crazy to tell them what to do. But I'd been forced into that crown – could it not be good for something? And Zayana didn't have to agree. She could refuse the request.

But I knew she wouldn't. Somehow, I knew she was the right fit for this. That she would be kind to these people as she'd been kind to me. Loyal to them. That she understood them. That she'd learned they could be more. This was the right choice.

"The Forbidding creeps across your land, swallowing up fields and farms, houses and villages, roads and harbors. How will you rid yourself of it?"

"There is no way to escape this dark magic," the woman in plate armor muttered after a moment where all were silent.

"Except that there is," I said, and I opened my palms and let my bees rush from them in a glorious cloud. How many had I let loose across Far Stones now? Hundreds? Thousands? And yet there were still more, rushing through me and out over the fields around us in every direction. Little scraps of me went out with them, torn from my soul in tiny bites. "But if you want me to give my life to help you escape it, then take this crown and honor my request."

I could already feel the Forbidding coming back for me.

"Pollinate hope," I whispered to my bees. "Change this land."

I was swallowed up so quickly that I could hear the cries of surprise from those around me – and then nothing.

CHAPTER FOURTEEN

Burn on our Pyre,

Bright and Hot,

Soul Made Naught.

Wait. Why was it quoting that to me now? I wasn't even back at the table yet. I certainly hadn't chosen another path. Had I run out of Aella to be sifted?

My heart hammered in my chest as I strained against the darkness trying to see. Trapped. I was trapped.

I was about to scream and then my eyes opened, and pain filled me, burning, burning, burning. The scream tore from my ready lips. I screwed my eyes up tight again, bucking and fighting against a prison that kept me from fleeing the agony.

When the pain dulled enough that I stopped, gasping in a breath, my eyes snapped open again.

My breath was ragged and fast.

I sat at the table. And I'd never be able to do anything else again. I was fully encased in the Forbidding from feet to neck. Only my head could move – and that only a little.

I swallowed. My throat was dry and with a lurch, I realized it would be dry now until I died. There would never be relief from that. I tried to cough and clear my throat as I looked around the table. The Raven and the Eagle and the Owl – Essena – and the Swan – Xectare – were entirely encased in the Forbidding. Only their faces showed. And those were frozen still as they looked at the board, fingers placed on the map for the rest of time.

I didn't want to look at Juste. I tried not to. But when I heard the keening moan coming from his direction, I knew he lived.

"I can't even touch the board if I want to," he said through clenched teeth in an aggrieved voice. "How can I finish the test, if there is no way to take the last step."

I finally risked a look at him and my stomach clenched.

His eyes were fixed on me. Not on the board. Not on the people stuck there. Not on the fact that one end of the room had broken open and the tangles of Forbidding reached inward from it, clawing at us.

Even now, even in this, he wanted someone else to bear the pain. To pay the price.

I looked away from him and out of that tangled end of the room and saw that it, too, was surrounded by the Forbidding – all except the dark stone mosaic of the floor. We'd been moved along the ground until we reached this room. All that swallowing had brought us into the belly of the earth, into the bowels of the Forbidding.

I shuddered. The cracks in the walls had formed a design that looked an awful lot like tangling snakes. The mosaic below us formed a pattern. And high above us was a wide glass window just like the one in the cathedral under the ground where Juste had hatched his snake for the first time.

It shone down on us, throwing red light over Juste's face and over mine, too. The image of a bird and a snake grappling each other seemed more fitting than ever before – and there, depicted in tiny glass fragments, were the bees.

Somehow, I was certain, the Forbidding had slowly moved us along to the hub, to this window, this matching cathedral.

We were back again to where we started – or to an iteration of it.

I felt ill. My head was swimming. I tried to call my bees, but my energy was spent. I couldn't even feel the heat in my leg from my wound there.

"This is the end," I said, more for myself than for Juste. I needed to stop hoping for a different outcome. I just needed to be strong for a little longer and then it would all be over. But I wasn't made for giving up. I wasn't made for surrender.

"What do you mean?" he asked.

"But only after they are sifted and tested, and the blood has been spilled and the sickness drawn out and the healing begun." I quoted the prophecy I'd seen in my memories as I still reached for my bees. I could almost feel them – just out of reach, just past my touch. So many thousands of them, so far away. I drifted on the thought, One with the swarm so far away. One of many – but still their queen.

"Blood," he muttered. "Blood spilled."

He fumbled as if he was trying to shake off his restraints. "What was that you quoted?"

"The prophecy about the Adder," I said. "They never expected us to live. It was always meant to be your blood here, Juste. Your blood spilled on this rock floor. It's what they were hoping for all along. They just had to make sure you were strong enough."

"Strong enough for what?" he asked.

"Strong enough to die."

He hissed and I couldn't tell if he was cursing or fighting or what he was doing. After a long moment, he turned his head back to me.

"Then why are you still here?"

"I don't know," I said, swallowing.

"Ask it to take you instead."

I laughed – a hollow, bitter laugh. Of course, that would be his request. If the world was ending, he would think that everyone would be wanting to see him saved from it. If there was one last glass of water in the land, he would be sure it was for him. Of course, it was the case here. The Forbidding had thought it could take his blood. It had badly misjudged the mark.

Ironically, it already had my blood on its rocks. It had been running from my wound for hours now – or possibly months. Time here meant nothing.

"Take me," I whispered.

YOU ARE NOT THE ADDER.

Juste looked up, twisting his head this way and that to try to see.

"Whose voice was that?" he asked, and he couldn't quite disguise the fear behind his rage.

"The Forbidding. It speaks to me sometimes. But it never says anything hopeful," I said, and I almost flinched at the resignation in my own voice.

Had I really lost the fight inside me? Please no, Aella. Please keep fighting. Remember who you are. You are relentless.

Juste turned back to me.

"Perhaps," he said in a low voice, "the Forbidding still fights on because it wants to have only one survivor. You've lived past your value, wife."

His snake struck so fast that I could barely react – but I did react, screwing my eyes shut and lashing back with my mind. When I opened my eyes a wave of bees was there, blocking the snake and channeling it away from me. Juste tried to strike again, his snake recoiling and then lunging, but again they turned it back.

He gasped, and again he struck.

And again.

And again.

My bees danced and I felt them as I felt my own body, moved with them as they moved, clustered and scattered, pushed and released, joining the intricate dance of the swarm. I was their queen, but I was also one of them. One voice in a chorus, one mind in a swarm, one beat in a collective heart.

The snake darted in from my right, curving to strike at my head. It was barely in my peripheral vision when my bees formed a cluster there, slowing it like a twig through mud and then bringing it to a stop. Juste roared and the adder drew back to him and then lightning-quick, it struck again – this time directly toward my face. My bees darted in from every direction and stopped it again. I felt my energy sapping with every block and every dodge, but there was nothing else for me – only this for as long as I could fight. For as long as I could live.

"It wasn't supposed to be like this," Juste said through his teeth as he struck and struck and struck looking for any weakness, any tiny gap of opportunity. "I had everything in place before I ever met the Hissan. They were just – the ultimate tool. The hidden hand. How could I not use them when I found them? It was the smart thing to do. My father couldn't defend against an attack he couldn't anticipate. My brother couldn't hold off a sea of dark magic on his own. It was the perfect plan. And then to add in this – mastery of the rest of this continent. I would have the greatest reign of any emperor in a thousand years. My name would be remembered forever. The Hissan even loved it – access to our Empire as my personal army. What wasn't there to love? And all that stands in my way is a stubborn wife. It will not be my blood on these rocks. It will not."

If I'd had any energy to spare, I might have shrugged. He'd danced us into this corner and now there was nothing we could do to fight it.

And still a tiny spark in me hoped he would die before me and I could still survive this. Hope is a mad thing. It keeps making you jump higher and go farther than it makes sense to go.

Eventually, the snake strikes grew slower and Juste slumped in his bonds.

"It won't have me," he whispered between attacks. "Won't have my blood. Won't."

I blinked and my head bobbed, and I realized I was dozing off. My throat was on fire with thirst. My belly hollow with hunger. I blinked and was awake again and I couldn't tell how much time had passed, only that Juste was still muttering, "Won't have my blood."

If only one of us was meant to be left, and Juste was the Adder, why was I still alive? Why hadn't it killed me yet?

I could feel my bees out there, scattered across the world, working and working, but I couldn't see through any of their individual eyes. I was too spent to even whisper to them. I just drifted in their warm buzz, letting my thoughts and heart drift in them as I moved in and out of waves of sleep.

"I will not give them what they want," Juste said and this time he sounded stronger. I blinked myself into full alertness and his eyes were fixed on mine – wide and bright. His voice hoarse. "I did not give my faher what he wanted – even when he put a sting into my vows, making it impossible to kill him with my own hand or to order any of my subjects to kill him for me. Ixtap was my solution to that. And now, if I can't give you in my stead, wife, I won't give myself either. Neither of us will escape this madness."

"I –" my voice came out as a croak and I tried to swallow to get some of it back. It hurt to swallow, the ache going all the way down through my throat. "I do not think we have much control of anything now, Juste Montpetit. We have been sifted down to the last."

He snorted. "You have no more agency, wife. And that is why you'll always be beneath me. You have never had the guts to do what I'll dare. And that is why you'll never fly so high."

His snake emerged from his mouth, sliding out and wreathing his shoulders, and when it was fully manifested he smiled grimly.

"I still determine my own path."

And then the snake wrapped around his throat and began to tighten. His face grew dark.

"I thought your own manifestation couldn't help you. You said that," I said. "You said that my bees couldn't heal me, so your snake shouldn't be able to hurt you!

And I didn't know why I was panicked. I wanted him dead, didn't I? As long as he lived, he threatened everything I loved. And yet seeing himself try to take his own life before me was too much, too wrong. I felt a desperate need to stop it.

"Please!" I begged. "Please, Juste. Don't do this. Don't just kill yourself to spite us. I thought you said you couldn't kill yourself with your own snake!"

I strained against my bonds with what little energy I had.

"Lied," he gasped, and then his face went red and his mouth opened as he choked.

In his eyes vindictive spite lurked with just a tiny hint of gleefulness. He loved this. He loved doing one last thing out of spite and fury. And even more than that, he loved having an audience for it.

"Please." I didn't know why I was still pleading with him. It did no good. There was steel in his eyes now. He was just as relentless as I was – but his relentlessness was bent to evil.

I shut my eyes as tight as they would go. I squeezed out every shred of light, my breath growing faster and faster and faster. I had thought his death would be a relief. It only left me hollow and full of regret. I kept my eyes closed tightly until the last gasp faded away.

CHAPTER FIFTEEN

I didn't expect to cry for Juste Montpetit. I had expected to feel nothing but relief when he finally passed to the next life and made me a widow.

I felt the moment that his soul left him. Maybe it was that feather in my chest releasing its hold. But I felt lighter. Easier.

I opened my eyes.

He was slumped in his bonds. His snake had vanished.

And I was trapped here in a room of corpses.

"I'll offer my blood," I said out loud. "I was wife to the Adder. I can offer my blood to the Forbidding."

There was no sound but the whistling of the wind in the room. I tilted my head back and looked up to where the darkness was beginning to blot out the light of the cathedral window.

"Hello?" I called.

After all, wasn't it done? Hadn't we made it to the end? There was no more sifting. No more weighing or measuring.

SIFTED.

The voice of the Forbidding was a whisper in my ear, barely even there, as if it, too, were dying.

AND FOUND WANTING.

Wait. It couldn't leave me here!

FOUND WANTING.

And then the voice was gone.

And I was still encased in my bonds.

Somehow, I had failed the test. I didn't even know how.

I drifted – sleeping perhaps, or simply fainting from lack of food and water. When I opened my eyes again, there was only the slightest shimmer of moonlight. In the faint half-light, I saw that Juste was completely encased in the Forbidding. Even his face was hidden. I would not be forced to watch him rot. A small mercy.

I drifted again.

My mind wandered and I let myself be taken on daydreams of Osprey and my family. It flitted from one happy scene to the next – dinner with my siblings, training wild horses and spinning to see Osprey there laughing and holding out his hand to me, chasing my nieces into the chicken yard as they laughed and squealed, giving one of my nephews a piggy-back ride as we went out together to check on the horses, watching Alect's eyes light happily as he scooped up a barn kitten, melting into a hot kiss with Osprey as the dawn rose around us.

Flight of Wings protect me. Mercy of the skies shine down on me. Give me peace to die well.

I was too late to save them from the Forbidding – but maybe I hadn't been too late to save them from the predations of the Winged Empire. Maybe that, at the very least, had been enough. Maybe they would grow and thrive as they could now that they were victors. Maybe they'd find their own way to fight back the dark magic of our continent.

Mercy of the skies give me peace. Lend me wings to climb to your rest.

I felt heat filling me, starting in my wrists and moving upward to sear through my heart. I let my eyes flicker open to where dawn was breaking golden and bright through the stained-glass window and through the cracks in the tangled Forbidding around us.

Mercy of the skies, I come to you. Do not turn my soul aside.

I drank in the light, drifting in the sound of my bees. They sounded busy. They sounded almost triumphant.

How long had I been drifting like this?

It was not the worst way to die. To come, at last, to the very end and drink the last cup.

The shreds of Forbidding forming the walls seemed to be drying out like husks. A wind blew through them and tiny wisps broke off, drifting through the room. I had to blink hard to keep my eyes clear of it. Little shreds even whirled off the sleeping figures around me. And where the shred broke free, small white flowers bloomed. Their hearts were gold and their petals white as snow.

Fold me under the shadow of your wings.

Tears stung my eyes as heat filled me and the buzz of my bees resounded through me like a second heartbeat. They were everywhere, through the whole world, through my mind and heart, through the spaces in between the light of the stars. Everywhere. Pollinating hope. Spreading life.

Above me, the window smashed, and tiny fragments of glass rained down on us.

The end was here.

I was too far gone to even gasp. Instead, I felt the corners of my lips turn up in a smile.

I was finally ready.

A dark shadow blotted out the warmth of the sun, descending down to me. My smile faded. I would miss the warmth of the sun. But the warmth in me was suddenly hotter than ever. Overwhelmingly hot. On fire. I was burning from it. Searing like a torch.

The heat was coming from the cuff on my right wrist.

My breath caught and my eyes adjusted to the light. He was there. Right in front of me, his chest heaving, his feet strong and sure on top of shards of glass as he crouched on the table map, looking down at me. Behind him, silhouetting him in purplish-white with sparkles of dust and dried Forbidding swirling around, was Os, his eyes flared with intensity.

And my Osprey's eyes brimmed over as his mouth dropped open.

"I'm not too late. I'm not," he breathed, and he seemed like he was speaking to himself and not to me.

It was only then that I realized the Forbidding was covering all of my face except my eyes.

He drew his sword from its sheath, biting his lip with the most heartbroken expression on his face.

He must be here to kill me. To shed my blood on the stones and cleanse the Forbidding. That made sense. And no wonder he looked so torn. No wonder he looked like someone was carving out his heart.

I was proud of him. He was relentless in doing good.

My eyes misted over, too. I was so proud. So incredibly proud.

I closed my eyes, waiting for the bite of the sword. And then opened them right away. I wanted to see his face as he slayed me. I wanted him to know I bore him no ill will. That I wasn't afraid to go and meet my mother and father in the skies beyond. That I wanted him to live and thrive and love again.

I smiled behind my veil.

And the clash that met my ears rang through my head like a bell. My smile faded and I gritted my teeth against the jarring pain. Flickers of Osprey's bright eyes and gritted teeth flashed between glimpses of his sword hacking all around me. I kept waiting for the pain to start, for the feeling of my life leaking from me to take over.

It didn't come. Instead, I heard a clang – as if Osprey had dropped his sword on the ground.

It was a dream, then. One more beautiful daydream of Osprey battling for me. One more look at his face before death's embrace took me. He wrenched at something in front of me and there was a sound like dry wood splitting and then the crunch of dried grass. I swayed – suddenly finding nothing holding me up – and collapsed.

Strong arms caught me before I hit the ground, cradling me into a warm embrace.

This dream was better than I thought I was capable of imagining. This dream was the best of them all.

I sighed, sinking into it. Death could take me now. I had seen my beloved one last time.

"House Apidae, you are so cold." His whisper was like music to my ears, lilting and strong, making all the little hairs stand up along my arms. "Here, drink this."

Something wet brushed my lips and I tried to reach for it, but my hands weren't listening to me. Water flowed into my mouth in a slow dribble and I drank it down. It felt like life itself. It was the sweetest thing I'd ever imagined. Nothing had ever tasted so good.

The water stopped flowing after a moment. I sighed, missing it already.

And then I felt his lips pressed against mine, fitting into them like a precise match and I had to revise my thoughts. No, this tasted better than the water. This was bliss itself.

I never wanted it to end. I felt hot tears flowing down my face.

Don't stop. Don't end. I'm not ready after all.

I opened my eyes and my heart lurched at the nearness of his closed eyes, his eyelashes like fans across his cheeks and his dark skin so close and so very warm and alive.

He was real. I could feel his breath over my face.

"My beloved. I knew I would find you," he said, and his eyes glowed with an emotion so much higher than anything I'd seen in them before. It took me a moment to place it. Devotion.

Relentless devotion.

"And though it took so many months of searching, your bees led the way."

He was real. I wasn't dying after all.

The tears flowed faster and hotter. I shuddered with relief.

"My hunter," I sighed as I tried to lean into the hand cupping my cheek. I wanted to do the same, but my hand would not lift – not even to caress him.

"In the end, they alone knew where you were – where their queen was."

"My bees?" I gasped.

The golden light was growing brighter around us and as I began to return to my senses, I realized they were my bees.

"They did it, House Apidae. They went all over the world and where they went the Forbidding bloomed. Have you ever seen a hundred thousand luminous white flowers before? They were everywhere. And where the flowers bloomed, the Forbidding withdrew. And we received our dead back to us one by one – all who had been swallowed up by the Forbidding were returned to us. Your sisters are back – the very ones I watched swallowed up by the flames of the Forbidding. I was there when Anfrea stumbled out of the white-flowered bowers. I was there when her children rushed into her arms. Do you know what it is like to receive someone back from the dead, my relentless girl? Do you know what it is like to know your beloved has healed the whole of the world and is still lost to you?" He leaned in so that he was whispering into my hair. "They tried to tell me not to come. But I could not leave you. Not then – not ever."

"Osprey," I gasped, and his lips were on mine again, searing and hot and so eager that my heart seemed to trip over itself in its hurry to rush to the next moment and the next.

One of his arms was under me and the other hand tangled into my hair, his fingers splaying through my tumbled curls, and in between kisses he would pull back and just look at me as if looking at my face was like drinking water after a day in the heat. I felt that, too. Every look in his eyes was like a new sunrise. Every time he smiled, the bow of his lips slightly swollen from kisses, it was like a new birth.

And wasn't it that?

Because moments ago, I thought I was dying, I was praying for the safety of my soul. And now, I was alive. I was in the arms of my beloved. I was free.

Something snapped beside us so loud that it sounded like a tree branch breaking from a mighty oak. Osprey's head tilted, his brow furrowing as if trying to determine what it was he was hearing. He pivoted, still clutching me to his chest – and then spun quickly in the other direction.

Something shoved him and he stumbled forward, gasping, fear in his eyes. I didn't have time to even ask what had happened before he set me – a little more roughly than I thought he usually would – on the litter-strewn floor and spun.

His back had a deep gash and blood flowed from it down the back of his jacket.

I gasped, my heart frozen in my chest. Standing in front of him, shaking off the last shell of the Forbidding – laced with tiny white flowers – was Juste Montpetit.

CHAPTER SIXTEEN

Juste shook himself and chunks of the Forbidding that had encased him fell to either side. They looked like torn pieces of a wasp's nest. My bees began to swirl, their golden bodies shimmering in the dawn.

Juste brandished his sword in one hand, wet with Osprey's blood.

I reached up to clutch at my chest, where his feather had been, but it was still cold to the touch. I ripped back my bodice to look at it. There was no feather anymore. It had vanished as easily as it had been bestowed. And, yet, he was standing there, sword in hand, grinning in a mocking way at Osprey.

"What did you expect me to do, brother? You were kissing my wife," he said.

A rumble rolled out of Osprey's chest as he snatched his short sword from the rubble beside him.

"I thought you were dead," Juste said, circling the table and keeping it between him and Osprey, as if he were buying time. "When my link to you vanished, I was certain it must be true. How else could you disappear like that? How else could you have ruined everything?"

My eyes fell on Xectare who was stirring in her bonds, her eyelids fluttering. White flowers bloomed on the edges of her restraints.

"Aella's bees are returning all our dead to us," Osprey said evenly as Os sprang into position at his back, ready, waiting.

"But you killed yourself," I gasped. "The Forbidding didn't kill you. You killed yourself. And it's only those who were taken by the Forbidding who are coming back."

"It's like you weren't even listening to the prophecies, wife," Juste said, reaching over to wrench a long strip of the wasp-nest desiccated Forbidding from Essena. Was that a mark on his back? A place where a wound had been? "Peace shall reign, and the dead will return. No one said anything about them having to die by the hand of the Forbidding."

But that wasn't right. I wracked my brain, trying to remember what I'd seen of the Hissan memories – but nothing came. The memories were gone.

My eyes widened, and as Xectare and Essena broke loose, I struggled – swaying – to my feet. I didn't have the strength for this. And Osprey was outnumbered.

He glanced back at me and caught my eye. "Stay behind me, Aella."

"You should go," I said, pulling myself up on a stone pedestal that looked like an altar. The room was different now that the Forbidding wasn't disguising all of it. And white flowers bloomed wherever the Forbidding was seen, lush and beautiful. They smelled of apple blossom. "You can still fly away, Osprey. There are too many of them to fight."

But before I was finished speaking, Juste leapt forward, his sword swift. He struck at Osprey and Osprey barely dodged, ducking to the side. His own sword came up to send the blow glancing to the side as he lunged forward.

Os screeched and rushed in front of him at the same moment that Juste threw up a hand. His green adder slid through his palm, darting toward Os, who stuck out his talons and grabbed the snake by the neck.

Os shook the adder as Juste roared, throwing himself at Osprey in a desperate lunge. His hands were as fast – faster than anything I'd ever seen. How was that possible when he had been dead? Shouldn't he be as weak as me?

They rolled, tumbling across the mosaic floor and coming to a stop over the head of a snake, tiled into the ground. And yes, there was a wound on Juste's back. And it was edged in black. Was it – could it be possible – that he hadn't died from his snake at all but from a stab by the Forbidding?

I shook my head. Now was not the time to contemplate these things or wonder how we could have failed the test if his blood really had been spilled on these rocks. It was done. We had failed. But we were back anyway and my bees had made it all possible. I didn't dare fail them now.

Beside me, there was another crack as the Eagle shook himself free, the Raven shaking free with him and for just a moment I could see all of this playing out in my head. I could see them swarming over us and killing Osprey – Osprey who had never done anything except love those weaker than him and fight with all his being to save them. Osprey who was my heart.

And they would sweep over me, too. I was so much weaker than them because I hadn't been frozen in time in the arms of the Forbidding, I'd slowly withered and faded and become nothing day by day, still alive in the grasp of the Forbidding.

I couldn't let them kill Osprey – and I couldn't let them spill out across the land as evil as the dark magic contained here, as much intent on twisting and destroying everything that came across their paths. I lifted my hands slowly and around me, the cloud of bees swelled – and then they shot out from me.

And we were one of heart and one of mine. We were the queen and the swarm, and we were one.

Wherever my bees touched the Forbidding, white flowers bloomed, springing fully to life in two blinks of an eye, their fragrance spilling out through the room.

They shot forward, cocooning the emerging Wings in a new kind of cloud – a cloud of bees. As hard as they fought, my bees fought harder.

I barely noticed Juste springing up onto Osprey's back his snake wrapping around my beloved's neck. Barely saw Os screaming down, his claws ripping at Juste's back.

I certainly didn't plan to kill. I'd never wanted to do that – not to anyone other than Juste. And even then, only to stop him from the evil he was planning.

But my focus was in a thousand places at once – in the eyes of a thousand bees, in the mind of my hive.

"What was done can be undone," Essena said, calling her bird up as my bees formed around her. "And not just here, but in the Empire, also. We four are enough to bring the Emperor home and set our reign in the heart of the land once more."

And that settled it.

"Sting," I whispered to my bees. "Sting with all your might."

And they fought for me as I stood swaying, channeling all my relentlessness into them. But this time it wasn't relentless fury that compelled them. It wasn't even relentless justice. It was love that sent them – love for my nieces and nephews, for Osprey's children, for my siblings, and for all the innocents out there who would suffer if these Wings lived. Love for freedom and the sun on my face without the fear of the Forbidding snatching me into its dark mass. Love for cities where truth could be spoken without tongues cut out, where fathers could defend children without being hanged, where people could protect the ones they loved.

And that love made my bees glow brighter and my heart fill fuller until the buzz and the hum and the dance was all I knew and I was one with the bees as they danced through the cathedral, as they pollinated the Forbidding and their flowers destroyed its dark tangle, as they stung those who meant us evil again and again, as they dodged and then swarmed, fled and then clustered around the spirit birds that kept flicking in and out of existence around the Wings.

And I did not revel in their screams. I did not enjoy watching those birds flicker out, one by one, those bodies collapse, one by one. But I did it because some things have to be defended. And sometimes that means you have to be the one who is willing to fight.

Essena leapt toward me. Behind her, Xectare was crawling across the floor. Neither of them got very far as my bees moved to two swarms, tightening around them and pouring into their eyes and ears until they opened their mouths to scream and the bees poured into them, too.

When they were done, I was left, heaving and dry retching, clinging to the stone altar as my bees returned to me.

I shook like a leaf trying to catch my bearings at the same moment that Juste stumbled into the altar I was clinging to.

Osprey's sword swept out, nearly slashing Juste's throat. Juste's snake reached above his head and twisted. Os screamed from above as the snake choked his life out and Osprey stumbled forward to one knee. His sword barely blocked Juste's arm. He was going to lose. He was …

No. I could do something.

"Sting, my swarm," I whispered and my bees shot upward, stinging the snake all along his green glowing spirit-body and then searching until they found his mouth and poured into it like honey.

Osprey cried out and I saw that Juste's sword had found its mark again, cutting deeply into his sword arm – he shifted it to his left hand just in time to turn the next blow, but he wasn't as deft with that hand and the defense was weak.

I glanced up again.

For a tiny, shivering moment, the scene above me was exactly like the scene in the stained-glass window as bird and snake fought with bees all around.

And then the snake winked out of existence.

And when I looked back again it was Juste stumbling this time – stumbling and falling right onto Osprey's quivering blade.

His eyes went wide as his blood splashed across the floor and up onto the altar.

"No," he gasped. And I didn't know if he was objecting to dying or to finally giving the Hissan what they wanted – his lifeblood on their altar.

But I would never have to ask. He crumpled to the floor, taking Osprey's short sword with him and when he slumped, his head was turned at an awkward angle and I could see death in his glassy eyes.

I was a widow again.

Chapter Seventeen

My bees swirled around me, exultant, delighted and across the room, I met Osprey's eyes, they echoed the mixture of sadness and victory that I was sure were filling mine. Bees were not complicated. They didn't feel pity and pain for enemies. But I did.

He stumbled to his feet. He was bleeding from arm and back, blood flowing down and his face was pale. I reached for him, but it was my bees who tumbled out of my hands.

"His wounds," I whispered to them. "Bind them up, close them, heal my loves, heal."

Someone cleared his throat and to my shock, the Hissan – Fierze, Lord of Asps, Radiant over the Crystal Caverns – strode in as if this place was his and we were visitors here. Had he been keeping vigil all this time? And if he had, why had he not left when we failed?

I fixed my eyes on him warily and Osprey yanked his sword out of Juste's corpse, shifting his stance to the ready.

Fierze ignored our body language as he looked around at the bodies and at Juste's blood spattered across the altar and then at me.

"It is done," he said. "There will be peace."

I wanted to tell him that he was a coward for sending us in

where he wouldn't go. I wanted to tell him that if the Hissan attacked us there would be no negotiating peace, that my bees would sting them out of existence. I wanted to tell him that the things you didn't pay for weren't really yours and that since this peace was bought with my blood it belonged to me and not to him. I wanted to say a lot of things. But my eyes were surprisingly blurry and Osprey's face was a picture of shock. I bit back my words and the war they might spark if I wasn't careful. If nothing else, months with no one to speak to had taught me how to be silent.

Fierze nodded as if he was satisfied and then paused. "Only do not come to our homes under the earth and we will not come to yours above it."

"Agreed," I said hoarsely.

He spun on his heels and left as if there was nothing more to say.

I let out a long sigh. It felt as if a heavy stone had been lifted from my chest.

It was done. It was all done.

And then, almost out of nowhere, Os dove down to where Osprey was, flying a circle around him and Osprey let out a startled laugh.

Like a knife cutting into a cheese, it broke down the crust of our sadness and my own heart bobbed up on a swell of relief. We were alive.

Feeding on that, feeling it with me, my bees swelled around me and lifted me up in a spiraling ascent, so that I didn't know if I was laughing or terrified as we burst through the broken stained glass window and into the sky.

I didn't care that my bees were unpredictable and that my strength was waning, I was only so, so glad, to be free of that place.

A purplish-white blur rushed by and then my bees caught up to it and we were one crazy gold and purple swirl, flying weightlessly through the air as Osprey reached for me. His hands found mine and the bone-deep feeling of home settled into me. Home was where he was. Home was where he smiled at me like that.

He drew me to him and tucked my head against his chest and the sound of his heartbeat was maddening in how it made me want to stay like this in his arms forever.

"It's over," he whispered before his lips found mine and purple and gold and soft kisses were all I knew. "The fight is over, Aella."

The fight, it turned out, was not entirely over, though it certainly seemed like it was for the hour that we drifted in the clouds in a swirl of purple and gold, until my bees grew weary and Os began to complain with little annoyed squawks.

I hadn't realized that Osprey was carrying me until we set down on a hillside and he leapt off Os' back with me in his arms. Around us, the land was covered in black, burned-out swaths, with a dusting of white flowers.

My bees blinked out of existence and exhaustion slammed into me as they left.

"So much destruction," I breathed.

Osprey shook his head, pulling a toothpick from the little packet in his sleeve. "You are relentless, House Apidae. But for just tonight, why don't you try turning that relentlessness into peacefulness. We are safe right now. And while I can't offer you much – I do have a pack stashed up here and in it is food and drink and a blanket. Why not live – just for tonight – in this moment? With me?"

I nodded and my head barely moved, I was so tired.

He carried me to a large half-burned tree. Chunks of it looked like they'd been hacked apart by an axe. Around us, the rocks were cut in oddly angular ways.

"All of this was swallowed up by the Forbidding before," he whispered around the toothpick bobbing between his lips. I loved that he still had that habit. It made him look brooding and predatory even when he was caring for me like a mother with one small child.

He set me at the base of the tree and reached around it to draw out a pack. He pulled a blanket from it and tucked it around me with so much loving care that I hardly knew what to say. We were on a rise and down below I could see the faintest outline of the spokes of the wheel, surrounded by gouges in the landscape and burnt swaths.

"And when your bees brought their pollination and changed everything, the Forbidding disappeared, but the scars from where it had been remain."

He pulled open his shirt and I saw his chest where my bees had burrowed in to heal him. There was a thick knot of a scar there, hard and round. And on his forearm, through the ripped jacket and shirt, I saw his new wound was thick with honeycomb and my buzzing bees. They didn't seem to bother him.

"The earth is marked, just as I bear scars and so do you." He tucked a hair behind my ear with a tremulous smile.

"We need to check your arm," I said, still surprised by how

weak my voice was. "And your back."

I moved to sit up, but he pressed me gently back.

"Aella," he said and it felt odd to hear my real name on his tongue instead of my nickname. "Wait. We should talk."

Something froze inside me, and I clutched at the blanket. I hated that I felt so weak, but I couldn't help it. I'd lost so much. And I'd thought … I'd thought I'd gained him back. But the way he was licking his lip and then biting down on it with those perfect teeth. The way he was looking off into the distance suddenly and then down at his hands and then up again. The way he couldn't quite meet my eyes with those gorgeous blue ones. It was making my stomach weave and flip.

"What is it?" I whispered.

He opened his mouth and then shut it again. And then opened it again. The tension seemed to stretch through the minutes until he spoke.

"When I first met you, I was the only person who was offering to help you among those who stole you away. And then you were forced to work with me to help the revolution. I hunted you for my brother. I fell in love with you." He glanced at me after that word – peeking out from under his long black lashes for a bare minute before looking shyly away again. His cheeks were flushed. "I've thought through every moment with you again and again over this past year."

"Year?" I gasped. So, it really was true.

"The year since you walked into the fires with him," he said finally meeting my eyes.

It had been an entire year. I could hardly believe it. Suspecting it was one thing. Hearing it confirmed was another.

"And after bringing to mind every moment with you – remembering it, treasuring it – it started to occur to me that you were thrown into this – into us. That you never really got a chance to choose if you really wanted this. I got caught up in joy back there. I shouldn't have kissed you like that. I should have given you space and time. I mean, look at you. You're half-starved and weak. You've been through so much and all of it alone. I swore I would come and find you and make sure you were safe and that after that I would give you time and let you decide and I'm sorry that I – "

And if he'd expected me to let him keep babbling nonsense like that, he had forgotten some pretty key points in all those memories of his.

With a snarl, I gathered up all the energy I had left and dove at him, knocking him back violently into the soft black ash and sealing my lips over his and I did not let him get up for long minutes as I forced the last energy I had to show the passion I felt. I caressed his face with one hand as I kissed him, memorizing the feel of him that I thought I'd never feel again. I let my hands stroke that dark hair of his, melting at the sweet scent of cedar and woodsmoke that tangled around him and when I really couldn't hold on to consciousness for even a moment more, I broke away.

I caught his gaze in mine and narrowed my eyes, threateningly.

"You're the biggest fool in the world, Vasyklo Petren of House Osprey," I whispered. "If you think I don't love you with every beat of my heart. And if you aren't here when I wake up, I will hunt you down and then you'll know what it feels like to fall madly in love with your hunter. And you will know why my family's battle cry is 'Relentless.'"

But I really was too worn out, because the last few words came out garbled and the whole world turned black.

Chapter Eighteen

I woke to the sound of bird song and to my utter shock I was not on the burned-out hillside. I was lying in a bed. Or rather – I was lying on an old straw tick mattress wrapped up in Osprey's blanket, but it felt like a bed. It felt like heaven after everything I'd been through. Even better, the ruined cabin I was lying in was completely missing one wall and that wall looked out over rocky mountains.

The birds singing so very sweetly made me feel safe in a way I could hardly describe. Safe to my very bones. I blinked back tears of relief – would I ever stop feeling like the whole world was a marvel and living in it was an indescribable gift?

Something warm was at my back. I melted into that good feeling of heat and nearby I heard a fire crackling in the old hearth. I shifted and realized that the warm thing behind me was alive when it shifted, too.

My heart leapt in my throat as I turned over and found Osprey beside me. His eyes were closed, his mouth partially open and his injured arm flung over his head. Had he bled too much? Was he unconscious? Had my bees done more than fix his wounds?

I sat up, my breath speeding as my hands flew to inspect the wound in his arm. But no. It was fine. New skin was healing over with just the faintest hint of honeycomb in the deepest part of the injury. It wasn't angry or inflamed and my bees were gone. Perhaps his back injury was worse?

I tried to ease him over so I could look at his back and his eyes flickered open. He'd only been sleeping.

I let out a shuddering breath, letting my hand rise to cover my mouth. Just sleeping, Aella. Only sleeping.

Those big arms reached out and gathered me close and he spoke muzzily into my hair.

"I do that, too," his voice was thick with sleep, as he rubbed my arm to comfort me. "A month after the battle of Karkatua I saw a man slip in the mud on the street and it was like I was on the battlefield all over again watching my friends slip into the mud and never stand again. I panicked, and Os shot out and caught his fall. The poor man was so bewildered he didn't know what to make of it." He nuzzled his nose against the top of my head and heat pooled in my belly at the closeness and the absolutely easy way his hand moved to drape over my waist. "We had to clear all the trees far back from your sister Helissa's home. She can't look at a waving tree branch without breaking out into hysterical sobs. They blindfold her when they take her places. It's easier for her if she can't see them. And Anfrea can't light the fires herself. Not since she died in one. We all have things we bear now, House Apidae. Scars that run soul deep. The Forbidding is gone but there will always be echoes of it inside us."

I cuddled in closer to him.

"I'm sorry I woke you." I had a voice again. It was a bit rough and sore, but I had one. I had so many things this morning. Even birdsong.

"I'm not." I felt a kiss on my forehead. "After you passed out, I had to rest for a bit but when Os recovered, I flew you here.

It's a hunting cabin, I think. One wall was torn out when the Forbidding took over this mountain. I don't know who owned it – Imperial or Hissan. But it was the closest place I could find with a bed and a fireplace. And even better, there's a spring behind the house. You can wash and get warm again."

I felt my cheeks grow hot at that. I was a mess. And I was still wearing the tattered remnants of the dress Juste had stolen me away in a year ago.

"I am a disaster," I said, looking down at my tattered dress.

"What was the dress for?" he asked and I could see the sorrow behind his eyes. He knew I wouldn't have been wearing this for any good reason.

"The coronation," I said. "Juste had it made for when they crowned me Empress. He put the Winged Crown on my head and he wore a serpent crown designed by Ixtap of the Hissan."

Osprey nodded and there was something deeper behind his eyes that worried me. "The crown he was wearing when I killed him."

I nodded, putting my hand gently on his arm. "Are you upset that you had to fight and kill him?"

He shook his head but that look of pain deepened. He winked suddenly – that odd wink of his that meant bad things rather than mischief.

"I am upset that I wanted it so badly. I'm upset at the relief I feel at his death – as if finally, I am safe. I am upset that I'd gladly kill him again and again to keep innocents safe. I am upset that inside, I am still a monster."

"I don't think you should be sad about that. And I don't think you are a monster. The monsters are the people who don't stand up for the innocent. The ones who won't speak or act because they're waiting for an easier way or someone else to do it for them," I said, shifting so I was on my belly, leaning on my forearms and I could look at him sprawled there. He was worn, I realized. There were lines on his face that hadn't been there before. A scar that ran down the side of his face from forehead to jaw. I traced it with a finger.

"But where is your crown, House Apidae?" His lips turned up in a smirk. "And should I be bowing now and calling you Empress?"

"I asked the people fighting on the mainland to make Zayana Empress and I gave them my crown," I said, feeling my cheeks grow hot. "I … I … um, are you upset Osprey? I thought you didn't want the crown, but I didn't ask you before I did that. It was yours to turn down."

My face was hotter now as I realized with horror that I'd taken that from him without a thought. It was his right to refuse the crown. I ducked my head, hiding my face from him.

Gentle hands turned it back up and I bit my lip as I watched his face through the fall of my tumbled curls.

His expression was blazing with something – something I'd seen so rarely that it was hard for me to identify.

"My Aella of House Shrike, now of House Apidae," he said formally and there was a teasing in his eyes. "Former Empress of the Winged Empire. The crown was yours to give as you wished. And I can only say that I am grateful you did not put that terrible burden on me – to rule an empire I still hate from a throne that never gave me anything but cruelty and pain. If you had named me Emperor, I would not have denied you for I can deny you nothing, but it would have eaten my soul out bit by bit. Let us hope it does not eat your brother's soul away. I've come to almost like that fool of a Shrike."

"My brother?"

He laughed, deep and long. "Well, Retger married Zayana in a hurried ceremony right before the Battle of Karkatua. And when the missive came from the Empire begging for peace and for Zayana to sit the throne, she could not go without him. I had no idea that was you, by the way, but I should have known – it was such a clever solution." His lopsided grin grew larger. "At any rate, I've never seen a man swear so much in my life. The air around Retger was bluer than the coats of the Claws who came to retrieve his wife for the task. It was all we could do to keep our boys from tearing them to pieces – and they knew it. They stuck together like a line of ducklings, their eyes wide and knuckles white on their hilts, but there was no blood spilled. And Zayana tilted her imperious chin up and told Retger he could do as he pleased, and she certainly wouldn't tie him to an Empire he hated but that her duty was clear. And besides, she missed her sister. And she'd seen a cardinal that morning with the sun flaring behind it like a golden crown, so how could he not see this was part of the world's grand design? What was he supposed to say to that?"

I laughed with him at that, shaking my head a little ruefully. My poor brother. He would certainly let me know how furious he was when he saw me again.

"He must hate me," I said, looking down again to hide my embarrassment.

Again, hands reached to gently lift my face and look into my eyes, but this time he kept his hand around my face, cradling it as he spoke and leaning in just a little as if to welcome me closer.

"When he finds that you live, hate will be the furthest thing from his mind. They gave you up for dead, my honeybee, and they said prayers for you. There will be nothing but joy from them when they realize you live. Just as there is nothing but joy for me."

His hands left my face and reached for my hand instead. Without a word, just with a faint smile and the pull of his hand, he helped me up and guided me through the back of the cabin and out a rickety porch to where a natural spring bubbled behind the cabin.

"I've already drawn water for drinking," he said, "and my spare trousers and tunic are on the railing."

He pointed to where they hung over the rail, blowing in the breeze. He let go of my hand and I walked down the steps to lean toward the water and touch it. It was icy cold – and yet, just being able to touch water again was a thing I hadn't expected to be able to do. It filled me with something that burned inside. Not rage – but relentless hope.

"The water isn't very warm," he said apologetically. "But I'll build up the fire and brew some tea and wait for you inside."

"You don't want to bathe, too?" I asked innocently, wondering what he'd do. He was far too honorable to join me in the water – not when we weren't married. Not when he saw me as vulnerable.

His cheeks flared with heat and his head ducked down. After a moment he cleared his throat.

"I'll just be inside building up the fire."

Was that a strangled note I heard in his voice? It was all I could do not to laugh until after he'd shut the door.

Then I let it peal from my lips and if the bang I heard inside indicated how he was feeling then the frustration was mutual.

I shrugged off the scraps of dress I was still wearing. The golden silk was worn, dirty, and streaked in soot. What had once been the finest dress I could imagine, wasn't fit for the rag pile now. You couldn't even wash a floor with this. I shook my head, tossing it to the side and hurrying into the frigid pool. The only way to get into freezing water was to leap – like so many other things in life.

I'd been taking a lot of leaps.

I sat in the water as my body adjusted to the cold and the dirt slowly loosened and came away as I rubbed my skin briskly. What leap would I take next? If this was a story, they would say, "And she lived happily ever after" but no one ever said what that meant or how to do it.

I washed out my hair shocked by how much of it just came out in chunks – burned from my time in the fire. I didn't even realize that I was sitting chest-deep in the water sobbing, holding one chunk of hair in my hand until he waded in beside me. He was in his breeches still, but his shirt was off and I could see the scar where my bees had been and the feather tattoo, and all the other scars and marks on him. His arm and back were still healing with my bees' honeycomb in them. I might have admired his strong, clean lines under any other circumstances, but it was like some floodgate in my heart had opened and all the emotions I'd been holding in for months were pouring out at once. He sat down in front of me in the water and took the scrap of hair from my hand.

"You're beautiful," he murmured as he wet his handkerchief and cleaned my face with it. It was that lacey handkerchief he carried everywhere. "Fire can't mar you for long, House Apidae."

"Who … whose handkerchief is that?" I asked, my eyes narrowing. I wasn't so broken that I couldn't feel jealous.

He chuckled. "It was my mother's. One of the last things of hers that I have. Don't fret about your hair, House Apidae."

"I'm not," I said in a small voice.

He didn't ask me to explain.

He didn't make any demands at all, but he took my hand and held it firmly. And I knew he was breaking his own ethics to wade in here with me. And I also knew he'd break every rule in the world if it meant keeping me from pain.

"You bore so much to save so many people. You were the heart and soul of the revolution. Without you, we'd still be oppressed and tied to a cruel empire. I would be tied." He tapped his chest over the scar. "Just because you're paying a second time in grief doesn't take that victory away from you. It doesn't make you weak. It means you were strong enough not just to fight, but to feel."

Tears streamed down my face, triggered by his words, shaking me silently with the truth of them. I had been strong for so long that I didn't know how to be anything else. I'd been fighting for so long that I didn't know anything else. I wasn't even sure how to breathe without all that rage inside me.

After a little while, he got out and found the blanket from the bed and offered it to me as a towel. And he was still just as careful not to peek as I stood up in the pool and took the blanket and wrapped it around me. But his face burned hot and it made something hot flare to life in my belly as I dressed in his spare tunic and trousers while his back was turned. A wicked part of me wanted to keep teasing him, even while the rest of me realized how precious it was that after all that had happened he still had this one innocent streak that no one had stolen from him.

I'd never been particularly delicate in my build, but I was swimming in the shoulders of his shirt even if the breeches actually fit quite well.

"You can turn around now," I offered, holding out the blanket and he took it with an embarrassed smile, wound it around his hips, and shucked off his sopping wet pants.

"You shouldn't have soaked those," I said with a wavering laugh. Everything seemed funny after all those tears – even a silly thing like the delight of my heart being too modest to skinny dip with me.

"They'll dry," he said, laughing with me. "Come sit by the fire and let's look at your hair."

The cabin had a fireplace with a wide, semi-circle hearth. I perched on the edge of it and brewed the tea as Osprey retrieved a dagger as long as his hand and set to work on my hair.

"A lot of it is burned," he said sadly. "I hope you aren't too upset that I have to cut so much of it."

He was cutting handfuls in little swaths and setting them in a mossy bucket he'd found somewhere. It looked like all of my hair, though I'd noticed he hadn't had to cut higher than my chin at any point. My curls sprang up when he sawed off the burned sections, spiraling out wildly around me. I wondered if I looked like Retger like this. Maybe I should tie it back into a tail like he sometimes did.

When Osprey was done he stood back and crossed his arms, inspecting me. And now it was my cheeks flaming hot and bright because I'd never expected to be examined by a man holding a huge knife and wearing only a damp blanket.

"I like that," he said eventually. "Maybe even more than before."

I smirked. "Only because you're the one who cut it."

"Well, I could have asked Os," he admitted. "But Os has very little patience. He would have just taken you out soaring instead."

I opened my palm and one of my bees tumbled into it.

"What am I going to do with you now?" I asked my bee, but my eyes were on Osprey. "What are you going to do with Os?"

"What do you mean?" he moved to sit beside me on the hearth, drawing a battered tin mug from his pack for our tea.

"We have all this power … but I don't want to rule, Osprey. I don't want to lead."

"What do you want?" he asked, offering me the tea.

I took a sip and then handed it back to him.

"I want a house far from people in the forest. And I want to hear children laughing. And tame horses. And tend bees."

He was silent for so long, sipping his tea, that I grew nervous. Would he judge me for my simple wants? What would he say about them? That I was being selfish?

And what did he want? What if he didn't want to live in the forest? What if he hated horses?

I couldn't take the silence anymore.

"What do you want?" I asked him, nervously.

Osprey caught my gaze in his, looked into my eyes for a very long time, and then finally spoke.

"You, Aella of House Apidae. I want you. And if there is a homestead in the forest and some children and horses and bees, then I want those things, too. And so does Os. We've never tamed horses before. I think he'd like to race them."

His eyes were dancing and his smile practically glowing and mine glowed with it. He reached into his jacket and pulled out a toothpick and jammed it between his teeth, looking at me with a rakish grin.

"That sounds perfect," I said, laughing at his expression. "I can't think of one thing to make it better."

He tilted his head slightly, as if disagreeing with me.

"You can?" There was a bit of a bite to my words – a challenge. After all, they did call me relentless.

"A marriage bond might be nice," he said with one of his deadly serious winks. "If you'll have me."

I winked back, slow and deliberate.

"Only if you give me one of those toothpicks," I replied.

It turned out that he was fine with that bargain.

CHAPTER NINETEEN

It was morning, before our things were properly dry again. We'd slept sitting up, cuddled together and leaning against the stone hearth. With no blanket, and one wall missing on the cabin, the bed was far too cold to sleep there.

"It's not a long journey home," Osprey said, wrapping his arms around me from behind so that I was tucked in tight against his warm body. He'd donned his dry shirt and dried trousers and his cloak was wrapped around us both. "It took me a long time to find you because no one had any idea what path you took, and the Forbidding was on fire or covered in flowers. All the trails and gaps in it were gone. The monks of Glorious Ingvar even say their tower there is no more. But the actual journey is not so long as you might fear since we can fly."

"How did Victore take that?" I asked. "He lived in that prison for a very long time."

Osprey chuckled. "He took it well. Oddly enough, he is building a physical tower in its place as part of the defenses of Glorious Ingvar. It seems the mind can sometimes heal if given the time and freedom to do so."

"Are you saying he's sane again?" I asked with a smile.

"I'm not sure he's ever been sane. But he's coherent. He knows where he is and what he is doing. He led us to decisive victories in the revolution. The people admire him. Respect him. He has a home in Glorious Ingvar – though the name of that city has been changed."

"To what?" I turned in his arms, surprised by his small smile.

"Victoretown. They honor him."

My eyebrows rose, but with my face turned I was distracted by his lips so near mine and for a few minutes we both fell into the kind of activity that doesn't allow talking.

"I stashed supplies at a spot about a day's flight from here," Osprey said eventually. "If you feel up to it, we'll fly there today. I think you need a proper meal."

"I would like that," I said, leaning in to steal another kiss.

We stood, stretching our legs, still huddled together in Osprey's cloak. He lifted his small pack, drained now of almost everything except a waterskin, blanket, and fire-making tools.

"Tell me about your journey here and I will tell you mine," I said as he flicked a wrist and Os materialized.

Os hovered above Osprey, cooing, flapping, and grooming him with his beak, and then – to my shock – he did the same to me.

"Did you know," Osprey asked lightly – but there was pride in his eyes as he spoke, "that Wings almost never marry? And especially not to each other. But I met a pair once. And the bond they shared changed their manifestations."

"Changed how?" I asked, as my bees whirled from my hands – just a tiny cloud. Just a few. And yet I felt more whole when they were there.

"They seemed to adapt to one another – to be able to work

together. To adopt some of each other's instincts."

"Are you saying Os might buzz?" I teased.

"Maybe I'm hoping for no more bee stings." But his smile took the bite out of his words.

"I don't think you are," I said, kissing him playfully and letting the bees out to play. They stung us both as we kissed, our lips honey-sweet as they clung together, our future brighter than the sun shining through fresh honey.

When I pulled back, he was laughing. He jammed a toothpick between his lips and offered one to me. I took it and put it between my teeth. I still didn't see why he liked these things so much, but there was something about accepting one from him that made me feel part of his life in a deeper way.

"Let's fly, House Apidae," he said, and he gathered me in his arms and leapt onto Os's back.

Os sped from the hill, seeming to grow as he hit a bank of clouds, as if he were as excited to fly as his manifestor.

"We've been flying for months looking for you. Just Os and me," Osprey said, but he didn't sound sad, he sounded content. "I'd fly to the ends of the earth if I knew you were out there somewhere, House Apidae. I would spill the last drops of my blood and shed my last hot tear for you."

I turned to look back at him. "But will you tether yourself to one boring place and live a quiet life there with me?"

He laughed. "You make it sound like a hardship instead of the one thing I've been dreaming of all these long lonely months. Come, House Apidae, tell me your story. What have you been dreaming of?"

So, as we flew, I told him about dreaming of him as I thought I was dying. And then I went back to the last time I saw him in the flesh in that house in the gap in the Forbidding and I told my tale – of revolutionary action and betrayal, of being put in a cage and being crowned, of being dragged to the fires of the Forbidding and sucked of my strength by his brother, of traveling to this far place and going into the last testing and the sifting.

He listened to me, pausing only to ask questions about the details. We stopped at noon to stretch our legs in a patch of forest that hadn't burned. I was still shocked by how much of the land was a black wasteland.

"Will we ever get it all back?" I asked, wrapping my arms around me protectively. I could still feel the lick of those flames around me, the panic of those who had been there with me, the deaths of all those who took that walk with Juste and me. What had happened to the other Claws who had been "kept" by the Hissan? I only felt grief when I thought of them.

And that made me think of the battles back at our cities. Of those who had died fighting for freedom or for loyalty to the crown – people on both sides. People who weren't all Juste Montpetit. People on our side who just wanted to protect their families and be free. People on their side who could only see one perspective and thought they owned our lives and futures. It had all been madness and lives lost and sorrows made.

I didn't feel the tears rolling down my face until I felt Osprey wiping them away. He leaned in close, his expression tender.

"For many days and weeks, your bees worked to repair in me what was broken. And they were magical. Who knows how long it will take to weave you back together, House Apidae? But I will be here to hold you in the darkness and wipe away your tears no matter how long it takes. Just as you were relentless in buying our futures, I will be relentless in fighting for yours."

And I believed him. And it made me feel light and buoyant inside as we leapt back onto Os and flew to the place Osprey had stocked and readied for us. Another tiny cabin in the woods, and then the next two days out over the burned landscape and sharp teeth of the mountains to a place tucked away in a little spot between mountains where smoke spiraled into the sky like a steely pillar.

"The first settlement reaching out into the Forbidding," Osprey whispered to me as we neared it. "Your people are made of stern stuff to come so far so very quickly."

I gasped as it came into view. I hadn't expected a homestead house all the way out here, just three day's flight from where I'd been held … and people!

They hurried out to us as we descended in the gathering darkness and there was such a blur of names and faces that I could hardly keep track of them all.

"We're the new outpost of 'Far Mountains,'" one of the children told me delightedly. There had to be a dozen children all running around underfoot with dogs and chickens and even a goat chasing after them.

A woman hustled us to a long table with benches on either side while another one set out bread and soup for us. I should have been paying attention to everything they were saying, but my belly rumbled treacherously, and Osprey pushed the soup closer.

"Eat, House Apidae," he said and then turned to talk to the twenty or so adults gathering around us.

"She's hardly eaten in months," he explained as if this was a normal thing, and then I lost track of what they were saying as I ate and drank, just so grateful to have real food in me again.

The food made me sleepy and my eyelids were drooping when a familiar voice surprised me. I looked up.

"Marcel?"

It really was the Single Wing blacksmith who had helped us find the gap and my family. To my shock, he was pushing his way through the people gathered around us, dragging a wispy looking woman about my age through the crowd. She had features similar to Zayana and dark brown eyes like hers, but her hair was white as snow and her eyes were faraway and distant instead of sharp and demanding. A tiny spirit bird the size and shape of a chickadee stood on top of her head as if she had put it there and then absentmindedly forgotten it.

"The moment they told me that a strange pair were here, clinging to each other like lichen to a rock, I knew it would be you," Marcel said, shaking his head and looking grim. "I told you that you should see a Skybinder then, and I'm saying it now. It is time and past time the pair of you were decently wed."

"What are you doing here, Marcel?" I asked in delight. "I was worried you had been lost in the gap."

He shook his head, snorting. "I'm too tough for that, young girl. I was out at the taking of Karkatua when the Forbidding lit like a torch. I was fine. But I never really took to the city life and when this bunch decided to do the unthinkable – to go to one of the places that Osprey here said was the most habitable deep into unknown territory, well, I had to ask if they needed a blacksmith. And, of course, they did."

I exchanged a look of amusement with Osprey. Marcel hadn't changed at all.

"And who should I find out here but you two. Still unbound, even though you should have been months ago!"

"Oh, well," Osprey began, trying to calm him but Marcel waved his hands energetically.

"No. I'll hear no denials from you. Tell the truth. Do you love the girl?"

Osprey's small smile was warm as his eyes stayed locked on mine. "Till my last breath."

"And you – you crazy, violent woman. You love this man who has spent these last months searching for you?"

"Yes," I said and if my words weren't as fine as Osprey's, I hoped my actions would speak for me.

"Then, this nonsense ends now!" Marcel said. "No more tying each other up."

"It's not what you think," I protested.

"No more stabbing each other with knives!" I opened my mouth to protest again but he cut me off with more of that furious waving. "You'll both be bound decently right here and right now."

I opened my mouth again, but then I shut it with a click. Because while it might be nice to be bound in front of my family and friends, I had learned that nothing was certain, and time might suddenly run out. And I just wanted to marry Osprey while I still had the chance. I caught his eye and looked a question at him, and he took the toothpick out of his mouth long enough to lift one eyebrow at Marcel.

"Then why are you talking about it instead of doing it, Blacksmith?" he teased.

Marcel grunted and gestured for the wispy woman.

"Colette. Collette!"

She shook slightly, her eyes going from dreamy and distant to suddenly wide.

"I'm here," she squeaked.

"As our colony's Skybinder, it is your place to bless and bind these two willing hearts," he said grandly, taking her by the shoulders and placing her right in front of us, presumably so she would know who she was supposed to be binding. Then he glared at me. "Up now, girl!"

I stood hastily beside Osprey and found my fingers threading through his. This situation was … ridiculous and strange but also sweet in a way I couldn't quite describe. For too long, I'd had the feather of someone I hated in my chest. I couldn't be more pleased at the prospect of having Osprey's there.

"You are supposed to face each other," Marcel barked. "Has neither of you been to a binding before?"

We turned to one another and I felt my face heating. The people around us had grown quiet and they stared at us with various expressions ranging from amused to sentimental, forming a rough circle so everyone could see. I tried not to blush even harder at their looks. Instead, I fixed my eyes on Osprey as the dreamy Skybinder said her words and had us make our vows.

And as I vowed to be Osprey's wife for as long as we lived, to make a home for him, to pray to the skies for him, and to honor him with love and understanding, I just kept looking into those steady blue eyes and I knew that we really could do this. We could forge peace where there had been war. We could make a home where there had been oppression. We could build something new. And we could do it together.

And this time when someone put a feather over my heart, it didn't burn or hurt at all. It only felt like the warmth of our affection, the heated glances we sent back and forth, and the hot promise of shared futures.

And I never wanted it to stop feeling like that.

EPILOGUE

I liked high places now. Places where I could see all the land around me, and check to make sure that there was no Forbidding creeping back across the land. Every time I ventured into the forests, I was worried it might be around the next tree or boulder. Sometimes, I thought I would never be free of that fear and Osprey said I didn't need to be. That he feared the same thing. That it was a weight we bore so that those who followed after us never would have to bear it again.

I sat on my usual bench at the top of the highest hill in the region, looked over the blue hills and bluer sky, and remembered when he'd told me that. We'd been married four nights before and the glow of our shared delight was still surrounding me so that every time I caught sight of him, he seemed to be bathed in golden light. My cheeks were permanently pink from blushing so much and to my surprise, his were, too, and he wore that little almost-smile of his constantly. I still thrilled at his every touch and when his hand settled on my waist in a very intimate manner as we flew toward Victoretown, I bit my lip with nervous pleasure. We'd crossed the ocean bay and land to get there from a place far in the Forbidding and I almost felt like the queen of the sky with all the flying we'd been doing. But when I saw the city, I had trembled.

I recognized nothing. Half the city was torn apart and being rebuilt. The area around it was trampled flat, the trees pushed back, and shanties scattered across the mud around the river.

"They're rebuilding around the city. Making farms. Making homes. The shanties are temporary," Osprey had whispered to me, but all I could see was the horror. I kept looking around for the Forbidding to return, or the rebel armies.

"It's over, House Apidae," he had whispered to me. "You made it safe for everyone."

"Then why do I feel such a hole in my heart when I look at it?"

"Some people carry the weight so others don't have to," he had whispered to me. "We manifestors bring to life the spirits of our heart. And you manifested bees. Everyone was so shocked by it that no one ever stopped to ask why. Did you ask yourself why?"

"I thought it was because I was so angry," I whispered back.

"But I think it is because you always care about everyone else. You are never alone. You're connected to the swarm. You feel their hurts. You know their pains. You dream dreams for their futures."

But even with his kind words, I never quite felt right in any of the cities again. We'd stopped only briefly in Victoretown. Long enough to get word from Osprey's contacts there that my family was gathering for the Autumn Lights Festival in Far Reach. And then we were flying northeast together to join them.

The Single Wing in Victoretown had offered Osprey the governorship of Karkatua and the area surrounding it. He turned them down. It wasn't the only offer like that he'd receive in that first year. Everyone wanted him to work with them or over them. They wanted to give him everything short of the settlement itself and he always turned them down. It wasn't until someone came from the mainland during the next year's Hatching that I asked him if maybe he'd like to take them up on one of their offers. This one had been to lead a school of Wings in the Court of the Winged Empire at the request of Empress Zayana and her consort, Retger of House Shrike.

He'd only smiled his slight smile at me, his dark cheeks flushing. "I didn't ask for fame or renown, Aella, and I didn't want them. They made my life like walking through the Forbidding every day. Until I met you. Until you cut me free and healed my wounds and made me whole."

And then he'd stuck his toothpick back between his teeth and never mentioned it again.

By the time we reached Far Reach for the Autumn Lights Festival, I was nervous and bouncing. I wanted to see everyone. I wanted to see for myself that they were alive and safe and well. And yet, what if they blamed me for all that they'd suffered? What if they didn't see me as the same sister again? What if everything was different?

I didn't need to worry. Osprey set Os down a little way off from our family homestead. We walked hand in hand down the old winding trail – only this time, we didn't have to watch to make sure the Forbidding wasn't reaching for us. This time, the weapons we carried wouldn't need to be used at all.

When we turned the final corner on the road and the homestead leapt into view, I stumbled. It was like something straight out of my memory. Horses whickered from the barn as Alect called to my nephew Frost to close the stall. Havet – one of my other nephews was picking up refuse from around the yard and gathering tools that had been dropped during the day – my old job.

Golden light streamed from the small-paned windows of the

house, flooding the yard with dancing shadows. Someone had re-carved the Shrike above the door and it looked down on us, glaring defiance.

A shiver ran up my spine, and I half expected to see the old man come out of the house, roaring that it was dinner time and we were all late. Instead, it was Anfrea who opened the door and called that it was time to eat.

They hadn't seen us yet, and I paused on the path, drinking in the joy of home. Of family. Of memories. There were scars in the land around the homestead, and a chunk of the barn had clearly been rebuilt – the whitewash on the boards was new. The same was true for parts of the homestead. The Forbidding must have curled in on it when we'd all left.

But it was all patched and mended, now. Just like our lives.

We stole up to the house after the door was shut behind Havet, and part of me didn't know whether I should knock or just go in. It was all the same as it had always been. But I was different. And I was worried I couldn't fit when I wasn't the same person.

After a moment, I looked back at Osprey and he quirked a brow at me. Taking a big breath, I opened the doors and stepped back into my old life.

"Auntie Aella!" one of my nieces cried.

There was a clatter, and something smashed on the ground and to my surprise, Anfrea was staring at me with her mouth wide open, a bowl of mashed potatoes broken at her feet.

Everyone around her was frozen, not sure what to say between the potatoes and the bowl and me. There were tears running down her face as she shut her mouth with a click.

And then she gave a long, sobbing gasp, and ran forward to wrap me in her arms. Helissa was right behind her, exclaiming my name as her arms went around us both. And Raquella and Oska and Awet and then I lost track in the hugs and kisses and being passed from one person to another. We were all crying and talking and hugging at once.

Osprey and I were dragged to a bench and made to sit down and then piled in loose children and quizzed about our journey and what had happened and how had Osprey found me? And when we admitted we were married, there was an uproar of irritation that there had been no ceremony and no special clothing, no gifting of horses – as was our custom – or gifts for home-making. But there was deep joy behind all those objections. And deep happiness in the children who squirmed all over us, stealing any trinkets we carried and offering us treats from the table.

I shared a look with Osprey and we started to laugh and then we told our story.

Eventually, the whole family was fed and hugged and exhausted and the children were sent to bed and the hot drinks brought out and I sat drowsily and listened with simple joy as my family told me their stories, too. But it was the missing faces that hurt that night. It was Abghar who would never join us again. It was looking at his son – the spit and image of him – and thinking how he'd have to learn his father's ways from his uncles. It was Retger gone across the sea – and that was my fault for giving his beloved the kingdom. And it was the Old Man who should have lived to see us all succeed – to see us stand up against injustice just as he had hoped we would – stand and win.

And when eventually no one could keep their eyes open, we all cuddled up in blankets wherever we could find a space.

The children had the beds on the floor above us. Osprey and I claimed the hayloft over the barn and he whispered sweet words in my ears and told me there is nothing to ease the heart about those who passed quite like bringing new people into the world. And maybe we should give that a try. And try we did.

We went back to Far Port with Royn and Anfrea after that celebration and I got to meet Osprey's 'children' who were mostly grown now, except a handful in their late childhood. And I saw him anew through their eyes. They were strangers to him now, after so many years apart, and yet they were bound with ties forged in pain and darkness, in bonds made by sacrifice and hope. The older ones were raising the younger and there was some talk of returning to Canaht to look for their parents.

When we said our goodbyes to them, we found a place far from anyone else, on a tall, tall hill so I could see as far as I needed to, and Os could fly as free as he dared. The first thing we built was this very bench. And then came the homestead. And the beehives.

Before we started with the horses, we made the long trip across the sea and saw the courts of the Winged Empire with our own eyes and I assured myself that Zayana was steady and Retger was happy. And though he teased me mercilessly for engineering things in a way that forced him to live in Kestrel City, he did seem happy enough. He'd started his own metalcraft guild and while his wife ruled, he was deep in the belly of the city, making strange creations of metal the likes of which I'd never seen.

Osprey took me for a tour of the Empire in the way only a man who rode a bird could. And I saw the great wonders of the continent with its sprawling gardens that bloomed all year long, its bird paradises where a thousand breeds came to dwell, the ancient wonders of palaces and statues and Skybinderies. And we saw House Osprey on the edge of the angry grey sea.

But all things come to an end. And at long last, we returned to our homestead and brought back order to our garden and bees. And began to weave our own kind of happiness from strands of understanding and love, of hard work and patience, until the place became our home.

I was sitting on the bench, still pondering all these things when I heard a bird shriek.

I looked behind me in surprise and found Osprey there, trying to look innocent with a toothpick between his teeth and Os flying circle above him.

"Thinking, House Apidae?" he asked me. Though, in fairness, I was of House Osprey now.

"Yes," I told him, sweeping the horizon with my gaze one final time. I would never let the Forbidding return again. I would be relentless in my destruction of it. Always.

The secrets of that dark magic had died with it. Where it had come from, what it had meant to do and how it had come to be a living thing – all of that had died with that mass of judgment and destruction. But what had been born out of it was so much more precious. And my bees kept a close watch. They would be ready if it ever returned.

My bees swirled around me in a cloud of happy buzzing. They'd been happy since we left the cocoon in the Forbidding, and I thought they might be happy like this forever. I didn't even mind anymore that they followed me around everywhere, clouding behind me or swirling over my head. They seemed to feed off my happiness. But I had so much of that to give.

"Would you like to think of something new?" Osprey asked

me, his dark skin glowing in the golden light of my bees.

"And what is that?" I asked, turning back to him with a grin. My husband never offered me any idea that didn't turn out to be a very good one.

"I heard a rumor that someone found a Hissan ruin to the north. They said there are bees carved on the walls and I thought that you and I should go and check to see if it is true and if there's anything there to find."

"You want me to go on an adventure when I'm a month from giving birth?" I asked, showing him my round belly as if he didn't know very well it was there.

He smirked, pulled his toothpick from his lips, and tossed it aside so he could kiss me very thoroughly, and only when he was done did he say, "I don't think you'll ever be sick of adventures, House Apidae. Not even when you have a dozen babies filling this homestead of yours. And I'd never want my queen to miss out on a good adventure."

"Your queen?" I teased.

"Well, the bees do circle around you. I've decided it might be a fitting nickname." And he gave me one of his fierce winks and kissed me again.

And if I was only ever queen of the bees and his heart, that would be enough for me.

BEHIND THE SCENES

USA Today bestselling author, Sarah K. L. Wilson loves spinning a yarn and if it paints a magical new world, twists something old into something reborn, or makes your heart pound with excitement ... all the better. Sarah hails from the rocky Canadian Shield in Northern Ontario – learning patience and tenacity from the long months of icy cold – where she lives with her husband and two small boys. You might find her building fires in her woodstove and wishing she had a dragon handy to light them for her

Sarah would like to thank Barbara, Melissa and Eugenia for their incredible work in beta reading and proofreading this book. Without their big hearts and passion for stories, this book would not be the same.

Sarah has the deepest regard for the talent of her phenomenal artist Luciano Fleitas who created the gorgeous cover art that accompanies this book. Without his work, it would be so much harder to show off this story the way it deserves. She also wants to thank her editor, Melissa, who tried her best to make this book better. Any errors remaining are all Sarah's.

Thanks also to the Noble Order of Female Fantasy Authors who keep me sane – sort of. And for my beloved husband, Cale and sons Neville and Leif who are endlessly patient as I talk to them about bookish passions.

Visit my website for more information:

www.sarahklwilson.com

www.ingramcontent.com/pod-product-compliance
Lightning Source LLC
Chambersburg PA
CBHW070538310726
48982CB00010B/1404/J